Caffeine Ni

Face Down

Garry Bushell

Fiction aimed at the heart and the head...

Published by Caffeine Nights Publishing 2013

Copyright © Garry Bushell 2013

Garry Bushell has asserted his right under the Copyright, Designs and
Patents Act 1998 to be identified as the author of this work

Published in Great Britain by Caffeine Nights Publishing

www.caffeine-nights.com

British Library Cataloguing in Publication Data.
A CIP catalogue record for this book is available from the British Library

ISBN: 978-1-907565-54-0

Cover design by

Mark (Wills) Williams

Everything else by
Default, Luck and Accident

For Loolee – one in a million.

Acknowledgements

I'd like to thank Darren Laws and Caffeine Nights for publishing this book and John Blake and Rosie Virgo for getting behind the original novels. I'd also like to thank Peter Cox for his wisdom and foresight, Tania for putting up with me and the original Bushwhackers - Mr A and Mr B - for giving me the inspiration to write *The Face* in the first place. If I had a hat I'd also tip it to Colin Edmonds, Mick Pugh, Peter Carbery, Stuart James, Tommy Irwin, Jeff and Mick, my brother Terence and my dear friend the PM. Much love as always to my children – Julie, Danny, Robert, Jenna and Ciara.

Up the Addicks.

Face Down

1

Saturday September 29, 2012. Bolton, Greater Manchester. 6.15pm

There are times when sunset can't come quickly enough, when the skies darken prematurely and even the streets seem to resent the lingering inconvenience of daylight. I was three yards from the kebab shop when the heavens opened above me like a ruptured colostomy bag. I ducked inside, shook the rain from my Schott parka jacket, and nodded at Ferhat.

"Usual?" he asked, flashing a gob full of off-colour teeth more crooked than an MP's expenses. I gave him the thumbs up and stood back. Nice fella, but he needed to sort out them rotten Hampsteads. To tell you the truth, the paintwork in his little backstreet khazi was in no better nick. You would never have guessed he knocked out the best halep kebabs in Greater Manchester.

There were a few people ahead of me, including a striking brunette, just the right side of brassy. Probably a little shy of thirty with a cleavage that was hard to avoid. She had a figure that would make the local Mullah think twice about heading off for evening prayers. Her iPod was loud enough for me to hear that she was listening to UB40, although it looked to me that She Be more like 36 double D. That's the thing about these Northern birds, they tend to come with a decent upper balcony – just how I like 'em. And believe me, it has been a while. The last time I got hard I put it down to early onset rigor mortis.

She was checking me out but I didn't let on that I'd noticed. Instead, I picked up a copy of the *Express* from the counter, and started to casually flick through it. I stopped at the William Broadwick column, and was aware that Knockers was reading it over my shoulder. She was wearing enough Charlie Blue to stun a mosquito.

Broadwick's lead article was angry, articulate stuff. Britain's courts, emasculated by Brussels, traitor politicians and their bleeding heart allies in the media, had left the country a haven for criminals and yobs. Was it any wonder, the columnist thundered, that 'ordinary folk now felt that there was no justice, just US?'

Never afraid to recycle an old line, our Willie. "Hear, hear," Knockers said out loud, adding. "Oh, I'm sorry." She pulled out her earphones. "I didn't mean to read your paper."

"Be my guest," I said, handing it to her. "It ain't mine."

"Ta. I do like what Broadwick has to say, he seems in touch with the man in the street."

Which street? Bond Street? Pall Mall? Sloane Square? I'd heard him on the radio. Our Willie sounded as much like a man of the people as Cameron or Blair. Her accent, on the other hand, was pure Smithills, common as muck. Again, just how I like 'em.

"He certainly talks a good fight."

"Listen to this," she said: "Trendy lawyers and politicians have elevated the rights of criminal scum above those of the law-abiding citizen. This has created an imbalance that cannot be tolerated. It is an offence against nature, against logic and against society."

"It's hard to argue with…"

I grabbed her arm.

"Hey!"

"Shh. Stand still."

"OK everybody, this won't take long."

An unshaven slime-ball with a thin, unshaven, rodent face and long wet, matted hair had walked into the shop brandishing a machete that, like its owner, had seen better days. He looked like a pin-up boy for *Scumbag Monthly*. Motioning at the queue to move back, he walked up to the counter. The two Turks behind the jump eyed him with a mixture of anger and resignation.

"Empty the till and don't try anything funny," rat-face barked. His tone was nasal, whiney, his eyes wide. He was sweating like Lee Evans at the end of an arena gig.

Oytun, the younger, prouder man, glared, but his father Ferhat put a steadying arm on his shoulder. "No problem, sir. Just please keep calm."

Ferhat opened the till and produced a ten pound note, £30 in fivers, six pound coins and a handful of shrapnel.

"Is that it?" the robber sneered.

"We have not been open long."

"This ain't enough."

"It's all we have."

"Forty-six poxy quid? You piss-taking cunt. Empty your fuckin' pockets."

Ferhat pulled out a set of keys; Oytun, a few more coppers.

"Are you fucking sure?"

Ferhat shrugged. "We've only just opened, it's early," he said, almost apologetically.

"Shut it!" shouted the sweaty little creep. He poked his machete at the elderly bloke in front of me. "Right, you! Hand over your wallet!"

Reluctantly, the old boy complied. Then Sweaty turned on Knockers. "And you, girl, empty out your purse and take off all the bling. All of yer, gimme everything you've got. Now!"

I caught a blast of fetid breath and clocked his choppers which were in a worse state than Ferhat's. I've seen better teeth on an exhumed corpse. These fuckers would give Shane MacGowan nightmares, they looked like partially decomposed Quavers.

There was a flash of metal behind the yellow stumps – his tongue was pierced, and his neck crudely tattooed with 'Cut here'. Oh how I'd like to. He waved the machete under her chin.

I stepped forward, my legs slightly apart, with the weight on my back foot. "You don't wanna do that, mate," I said calmly.

The cocky little smack-head sneered. "Why, what are you gonna d...?"

Before he could finish the sentence, I grabbed the hand holding the tool and jerked it back until his wrist snapped. The jerk yelped in pain, dropping the machete. A good hard left to the guts doubled him up, and a right knocked him spark out. His body hit the floor and stayed there.

"Junkie slime," I muttered. The punters spontaneously clapped and cheered.

Oytun was straight on the blower to the Old Bill. Ferhat came over and started returning his customers' property, apologising profusely, and Knockers flung herself into my arms, which was nice.

"Thank you so much," she said. "That's the bravest thing anyone has ever done for me."

Her mouth looked soft and wet, extremely kissable.

"S'OK. You OK?"

She nodded. "I'm going to tell the local papers all about you."

"No you're not, darling. I'm going to collect me halep, say good night and go home."

"But you're a hero."

I flashed a smile that made her legs melt. "All the best heroes have alter-egos," I said with a wink.

She looked blank.

"You know, Clark Kent, Bruce Wayne, Peter Parker, Matt Murdoch... no relation to Rupert."

Blanker. I turned away.

"No hold on," she said. "I do get it. I just wouldn't open with it..."

Ho! She was funny as well as cute. I liked her even more. Ferhat defused the unresolved sexual tension.

"Thank you, H, thank you, so much" he said. "Here, your food is ready, it's on the house."

"Cheers, Ferhat. You sure? You don't have to, mate."

"Please, please, thank you so much."

"I'm Katie," said Knockers. "What's your name then? Just for me. I'd like to know who..."

"Who was that masked man?"

"You're not wearing a mask."

"I never leave home without one."

"Who are you, though?"

What could I tell her? That I call myself Harry Tyler and I'm a bastard? In fact I'm a bastard's bastard and I would break her heart as easily as I could have broken rat-boy's neck. Oh, and by the way, I don't tell anyone my real name because M15 want me dead?

I had too much history to even get started, so I just said "Really nice to meet you."

"Katie, I'm Katie."

"Yeah, you said, gorgeous. And I'm gone. Sayonara sweetheart."

I kissed her on the cheek, squeezing her arm just a moment too long, and walked out. It was still pissing down. Behind me, Ferhat happily grassed me up, volunteering the name and location of my local, the whereabouts of the backstreet boxing gym I occasionally train in, and the fact that I got a take-away from there once a week like clockwork.

"Be very wary of this man, miss," Oytun had said.

"Why?" she'd asked.

"He is a wrong'un. I have it on good authority that he supports West Ham."

Well, someone's got to.

2

Sunday, September 30, 2012. Royal Tunbridge Wells, Kent. 12.05am.

They say your life flashes before your eyes when you die, but that isn't strictly true. It's not the good memories that play back in the final moments before oblivion, not the love or the triumphs or the happy times. It's the pain and the let-downs, the failure and the regrets. The things you've done wrong.

The avenging angel watched Timothy Brown run, knowing that his last thoughts would be flashbacks of the suffering he'd caused. The faces of his victims – young, innocent faces, terrified, panicking and wracked with pain – would haunt the sick, dickless bastard all the way to eternal damnation.

Brown looked back and saw the gun in the angel's hand. Then the dirty nonce panicked, tripped and fell. The avenger was over him in a heartbeat. He opened his mouth to scream – but it was too late, the angelic finger had already pressed the trigger. He was holy toast. The angel nodded dispassionately.

No justice, just us.

3

Eleven hours later.

It was a day much like his ex-wife, cold and overcast, thought Mick Neale; but now he was in the pub he felt a lot happier. He generally did. He settled on his favourite bar stool, sipped his pint of lukewarm London Pride, winked at Thelma, and out of habit started assembling a Golden Virginia roll-up.

"DAD!" A young boy's voice disturbed the peace as rudely as a bugler at a séance.

"Is that your Mark?" asked Thelma.

"Yeah," Mick grunted. "It'll wait."

He picked up a discarded *Sun* and flicked through the sports pages. There was something very appealing about Thelma. She was sturdy but sexy, and the attraction was mutual. He could see it in the twinkle in her eyes, and feel it in the flirtatious sub-text every time they spoke. One date, tops, and he'd be in there like a pack of beagles. No crevice unsniffed.

"DAD!" The boy again; more urgent now. His shout was followed by a girl's scream. Mick threw down the paper and ran out of the Toad Rock Retreat. He could see the back of his son's head, up on the rocks.

"What is it?" Mick shouted. "This better be good, Marky."

"It's a body."

"What?"

Mick clambered up the damp, slippery rocks to where his ten-year-old was perched, and eased a younger, crying girl to one side. Other kids and a few parents were drawn towards the commotion.

Mick looked to where Mark was pointing and sucked in his breath. It was a body, all right. Face down, male, white, late twenties, brown hair, cheap clothes, old trainers. Slowly, he lowered himself down between the rocks. He started to take the man's pulse and recoiled.

"What...who?" The sobbing girl's mother had arrived, scarcely more collected than her daughter. "Has he slipped?" she said. Very jolly hockey-sticks. "Here, pass him up, I'll help."

"No point, he's dead."

"How can you tell?"

Mick looked up at her.

"The bullet hole in his forehead's a bit of a clue."

It was a clean wound, with a small, round abrasion collar and a 'tattoo' of powder markings around it. The back of his head was a mess. He'd been plugged from the front, straight on, at close range. Alongside the footprints of the corpse's trainers Mick noticed a trail of imprints, size eleven or twelve, coming and going in the mud. They looked like Doc Martens.

A couple of teenagers in Burberry caps leaned forward and started taking pictures with their mobile phones.

"For pity's sake," Mick snapped. "Give the man some dignity. Make yourself useful with them things, call the Feds."

He grabbed Mark by the arm and marched him back to the pub. A crowd had started to congregate at the foot of the rocks.

"Man, wha' happen?" said a pasty white teenager in a Dr Dre T-shirt, with a face like a marinara pizza.

"It's a body, like on CSI," shouted Mark.

"Cool," the little twat replied.

4

Nine hours later. Ongar, Essex.

Simon Loewy climbed off the girl and made a low guttural, animal sound. Like the pig he was, Lotte thought. Car sex, not exactly classy but at least the back of fat-boy's Bentley had more style than her old man's Transit van. She reached for a tissue and discreetly mopped a small pool of his drool off her neck and shoulder.

Loewy pulled off the condom with one hand, studied its contents absent-mindedly, and patted her leg with the other. He still had it. "Need a slash," he mumbled gruffly.

And they say romance is dead, thought Lotte.

Loewy opened the car door. It was raining stair rods. Bollocks. He lobbed the condom, and made a dash for the nearest tree. Charlotte shook her head and pulled her crepe de Chine panties back up. Poor old lover boy, she thought – out of shape, out of breath and out of time.

Loewy smirked. It had only taken him two dates to smash it, and he hadn't even had to shell out for a hotel room. Bargain. Strange girl. Quiet, face like porcelain. She'd just wandered into his shop one day and the old Loewy charm had done the rest. He could have made the sex last longer, should have done really, but it had been a long day. Still, he would see her again. She weren't a bad sort...a classy brunette with a cute smile and a lot of style. Lotta, that was her name. Or was it Liza? If it was Lezza he'd definitely have her again, and her friend. All he had to do now was figure out a way to get shot of her on the hurry-up. He shook off the final drips and jogged back to the car. Lotta or Leeza was reaching into the glove compartment. "Fuck me," he chortled. "It's pissing down like a cow with two cunts. If it rains any more they'll find Nemo. I was just, er…"

He spotted the Wildey pistol – *his* Wildey pistol – in her hand.

"Careful love, that thing's loaded."

She rang her small, neat pinky finger down the weapon, grazing the tip coquettishly.

"Something else with an eight-inch barrel."

Loewy chuckled. So pleased with himself, thought Lotte. Conceit – God's gift to little men.

"Is this for her indoors?" she asked with a grin. "Who needs divorce courts when you can just blow the bitch away, right?"

"Don't be daft," he smiled. "If it ever comes to that, I'll get a pro in."

"How about me?"

"You?"

"I can handle a gun."

"Ha! Who'd hire a woman hit-man?"

"Your wife," she lied.

Simon Loewy's face was frozen in a half laugh when the .449inch 240 grain bullet shot through his heart.

Straight to hell, boy; straight to hell, boy. "And may God have mercy upon your soul," muttered Lotte. She removed her ER20 ear defenders and began to stuff pages from a torn-up magazine into his open mouth. "Because no one else on His good green earth will."

She took out a packet of hygienic wipes from her handbag and cleaned her hands before thoroughly scrubbing clean every surface she might have touched. Then she scattered a handful of blonde hairs that she had picked up earlier at her local salon on the back of the passenger seat. The rain was finally stopping. She got out of the car and took one last look at Simon Loewy's corpse. It seemed even more blubbery and charmless in death than it had been in life. Thin lips, she thought. Never liked 'em. Never trust a man with thin lips.

5

Monday October 1. Buckinghamshire. 8.45am

Jackie Sutton ran her hand up William Broadwick's upper thigh, softly grazing his right testicle. He quickly brushed it away. What was wrong with the woman? He was forever telling her they had to be discreet in public and their train was packed with sullen Monday morning commuters. Jackie turned away and pretended to sulk. Broadwick buried his head in the *Times*. They'd been seeing each other on the sly for three months now. She was a secretary – sorry "executive assistant" – at a PR firm who worked for David Cameron's new Blairite Conservative Party. He was the author of the country's most determinedly right-wing newspaper column: Broadwick's Broadside, a weekly rant against the country's ceaseless descent into sopping wet social liberalism.

Broadwick's column, his no-nonsense radio talk show, and to a lesser extent his short-lived, critically-ridiculed satellite TV show had made him a hate-figure for the Left and an iconic figure (wags said "fuehrer") for the Thatcherite rump of the Tory Party, disenfranchised by their leadership's headless flight to the soggy centre on course for what William often called "Eurogeddon". Broadwick was the voice of reason; the voice of freedom, patriotism and family values – which was why he had to keep their affair firmly under wraps.

Jackie's mobile rang. If Broadwick had recognised the ring-tone, it might have disturbed him even more. It was Natasha Bedingfield's 'I Wanna Have Your Babies'.

She answered it eagerly.

"Hello...oh hi Mum...on a train...yes, coming back from Milton Keynes...business...yes, with Willie..."

Oh God. Broadwick glared at her angrily. A couple of young men in suits a few seats down had spotted him. This wouldn't do. He got up and walked out into the corridor and stood by the toilet, watching the Buckinghamshire countryside roll by. He looked at his Tag Heuer watch. It was 9am. Four hours 'til his deadline. He called the Editor.

"Paul? It's William. Just on my way in. Anything happening?"

"Two deaths," the Editor said gleefully. "Good ones too. There's been a paedophile murdered in Kent and a porn baron gunned down in Essex in his own car."

"Double bubble! Good riddance to both."

"My thoughts exactly. Will you say that?"

"Absolutely."

"Excellent. Right, well, we'll do a leader disassociating the paper from your views."

"Any other details known?"

"The paedo was one Timothy Brown. He raped an eleven year old boy in Hastings when he was 17, did eighteen months for that, and was recently released from prison early after two similar offences. Bit of an outcry in the local papers about that, apparently. His body was found dumped in some rocks the other side of Tonbridge. The porn baron was Simon Loewy. Scum of the earth, ran a chain of provincial shops in Essex and Hertfordshire, known links with organised crime; had been prosecuted and fined several times for supplying hardcore filth under the counter. You wrote about the travesty of his latest trial only last month."

"Of course!"

"Whoever killed him stuffed his mouth with pages torn from one of his own porn magazines, *Schoolgirl Bondage Sluts*."

"Poetic justice."

"Quite. They shot him through the heart."

"Who would have guessed he actually possessed one? That Brown case rings a bell as well, Paul, I..."

Jackie came through the doors, holding her bag and his briefcase. Broadwick held a finger to his lips. She nodded and walked ahead to the buffet car.

"I'll get cuts emailed through. OK, guv'nor, I'm about half an hour away."

"See you in the office, superstar."

He closed his phone. "Mr Broadwick?"

William looked at an elderly man in thick spectacles and a suit the colour of wet cement. He was smiling. A reader?

"Yes, how do you do."

"A pleasure to meet you, sir," the stranger said, proffering a limp hand. "David Graham. I've long been an admirer of your work."

"Thank you."

"I wondered, as a reader, how you would solve the problems of the railways. It strikes me the trains have been getting worse. They were bad when they were nationalised, but since they've been privatised standards of service have slipped even more."

William breathed in sharply and went into auto-rant mode. "You're absolutely right," he said. "The trains were useless when they were nationalised, and they're certainly no better now. The wrong kind of privatisation has just allowed a few greedy spivs to get richer out of our misery."

"So what's the answer?"

"Well, the first step would be for the government to extend standard franchise terms to twenty years, to encourage greater investment and stability."

"Yes, that's sensible."

"They should also encourage a major transfer of freight away from the roads and onto trains and canals and expand the rail network by re-opening lines where there is a proven need."

Jackie came back. He motioned to her and carried on, trying to conceal his relief. "Now if you'll excuse me, I have to talk to my PA."

"No, that's perfectly fine," the man replied. "Thank you so much for your time. You ought to go into politics, I often tell my wife that."

"Thank you, Mr Graham, pleasure to meet you."

"And brick up the Folkestone end of the Eurotunnel."

"Ha, ha, yes." Broadwick forced a laugh.

"You're so good with people," said Jackie, brushing the fine smattering of dandruff off his collar. "You really ought to go into politics, you know, he's right – you're a natural. You're like Simon Heffer with a non-toxic personality."

"Maybe, some day."

"I mean it," she said with feeling. "Everyday people are rudderless, they feel let down by conventional career politicians, and understandably so, because they have become a caste apart. You reach the common man, Willie, you could fill that vacuum."

"Hmmm," Broadwick replied. His face twisted into a sulk, his smile melting away like a Salvador Dali clock.

"All okay?" Jackie asked, sensing it wasn't.

"You really shouldn't talk to anyone about us, Jack."

"It was my mother."

"Secret means secret."

"Do you love me?"

"You know I think the world of you, but if any word of this gets out, I'll be crucified."

"I know, I understand. I'm not a bunny-boiler."

"I know." More of a slow-roaster, he thought.

"Come here."

She opened the toilet door and pulled him through. His protests stopped within ten seconds of her unzipping his flies. Her hand plunged in. He was hard almost instantly and when she took all of him into her mouth in one smooth and wonderful movement it was all he could do to stop himself from coming on the spot. His moans were coming out in spurts. William Boardwick lasted a full thirty seconds before Little Willie gratefully did the same. God, this girl was fantastic. His wife had never liked oral sex and wasn't any good at it. She sucked, in fact, but not in a good way.

William rested against the cubicle wall, beaming. Jackie pulled out some toilet paper and spat the great man's seed into it.

"That's better, Willie," she said. "Grumpy Mr Hyde is happy Doctor Jekyll again. Now give us a kiss."

"You're joking! I know where those lips have been."

She smiled. "I'll leave first. You give me a *head* start."

As Jackie slipped out, a young shaven-haired yob in paint and plaster-splattered work clothes came straight in.

"Oi Oi," he said. "Khazi for two, don't mind if I do."

The builder did a double take.

"Don't mind me, mate," he said. "Give her a broadside! She's well fit, innit?"

He slapped the columnist's back as he hurriedly left the toilet.

"See what I mean?" Broadwick hissed as her caught up with Jackie.

"He's a building worker, William, what harm can it do?"

"These things have a way of getting out."

The train pulled in to London Euston. Broadwick shot out and made for the cab rank. Jackie ran to keep up, tottering in her heels.

"Can you drop me off at Portland Square? I've got a 10 o'clock."

"Can't. I'm off in the opposite direction."

She shot him a look he could have shaved with.

"It's copy day!" the thunderer thundered.

"How about a drink in the Walrus after work?"

"I'll call you."

She went to kiss him on the lips. Broadwick pecked her cheek and jumped in a cab. As it drove off, Jackie waited for him to wave, but he was too busy picking the blonde hairs off his crotch.

6

Tuesday, October 2, 2012.8.30am.Kent.

There weren't many murders in Royal Tunbridge Wells. Certainly none like the execution of Tim Brown. Detective Inspector Gary Shaw knew that the rotten little toe-rag was no loss to the world, but even so, this was too much. Shaw's wife Joanne had led the Child Exploitation and Investigation Team which had collared Brown in 2010. He'd been bang to rights – guilty not just of "engaging in sexual activity" with eleven year old twins, a boy and girl, but of making indecent images of them. It was known locally as the Hansel and Gretel case because he'd lured them into his "candy-shack" flat on Halloween. There had been uproar when Brown had received a three year sentence and more when he had been released even earlier following a successful appeal based on minor technicalities.

Shaw called his team into the incident room at Tonbridge police station for the briefest of briefings. "Get me information on everyone who might have a grudge against Timothy Brown, including family and friends of the twins. Get me names of all his known associates, including any other creeps and sex offenders he was in touch with."

Shaw sipped his coffee, which was as tepid as a baby's bath water and did nothing to lift his mood. He turned to his Detective Sergeant, Rhona 'Wattsie' Watts. "Rhona, any word yet on the weapon?"

"Still waiting for forensics, guv."

"Well, put a rocket up their arse. The quicker we move on this, the better. The press are looking for someone to kick and I don't want it to be us. What else is there?"

"One vague eyewitness report of a man in a flat cap and Barbour jacket moving suspiciously, no other description; and the size 12 footprints, Airwair soles...Doctor Marten boots," replied DC John 'Womble' Piddlington, an overweight 35-year-old with breath that could strip wallpaper. "And that's it, guv."

"Age? Height? Colouring?"

"Nothing... except an old dear with insomnia saw a Land Rover driving away pretty sharpish at about the right time. She didn't see the plate."

"OK, check CCTV, just in case he came back through town. Pictures?"

DC Jim Woodward produced a see-through stud wallet containing the crime scene snaps. Shaw shifted through them absent-mindedly. If he were hoping for divine inspiration, none came. When the briefing was finished, Wattsie took him to one side.

"You seen the *Express* today, guv?" she asked.

"Nope."

She showed him the William Broadwick column. Shaw groaned as he read the relevant passage. 'I do not advocate vigilantism, but we should shed no tears for the likes of Brown and Loewy. There is no doubt Britain is a better, safer place without them. My only regret is that they didn't suffer as painfully as their victims.'

Gary Shaw shook his head. "This isn't helpful," he said.

"The man's a prick," Rhona Watts concurred.

7

Sunday October 7. Woking, Surrey. 10am.

William Broadwick settled outside the high street coffee bar with his small mountain of Sunday papers and a Jiffy bag full of his weekly mail from readers, some of it not scrawled in green ink. He generally avoided the high street during the week. It was always full of lumbering lard-arse punters, aggressive, feral kids and semi-bewildered ancients, many of whom, half-recognising him from his by-line picture, would attempt to strike up a mind-numbing conversation. But it was the bolshy white teenagers with their Jaifaican 'multi-ethnic yout' accents' – the wannabe gangstas – that got under his skin the most. This was Surrey, for God's sake, not the arse-end of Lambeth or the People's Republic of god-forsaken Newham. They were a lost generation. Nothing national service, the birch and a short war wouldn't put right, though.

Mercifully, Sundays were different, especially this early in the morning. There were fewer 'sheeple' about for a start, and when the sun was out, you could sit outside with a broadsheet, a Gauloise Disque Bleu and a freshly squeezed orange juice and feel almost continental.

Fiona had gone inside to order brunch. Broadwick stared with disdain as a pair of middle-aged women dressed like teenagers strolled past, their pierced navels on unattractive and unnecessary display. At least Fiona knew how to dress. His wife was effortlessly stylish. Even around the house, she looked classy in Tory Burch tunics and £150 Habitual jeans. He began to flick through the *Sunday Telegraph*.

"Mr Broadwick?"

With half a sigh, Broadwick looked up at the unshaven man rapidly moving into his personal space. He smiled warily.

"I thought so. I liked the piece you wrote on refuse collections last week. Of course they should be weekly."

Broadwick nodded vigorously, another satisfied customer.

"It's outrageous," he said. "It's been the British householder's right to have a weekly waste collection since Disraeli."

"There has to be weekly collections," the man continued. "Otherwise there would be huge mounds of filth accumulating on our streets…"

"Yes, yes."

"By which I mean discarded William Broadwick columns. You are one sick old bastard."

"What?"

"That column of yours, it's fascist filth. Last week you were virtually encouraging people to attack anyone they suspected of being a paedophile."

The man's face had suddenly become as cold and hard as an ice queen's nipples. Broadwick switched immediately into attack mode.

"Our laughable justice system leaves these animals walking the street," he said, raising his voice angrily.

"So fight to change the law, don't encourage lynch mobs."

Broadwick glared at him. "That's easy for you to say," he retorted. "But this particular scumbag, Brown, had struck before, and was freed to strike again because of our toy-town courts – and the 'law' that you obviously look up to has become so perverted by grasping left-wing lawyers that it has become a tool to beat the honest and hard-working. No wonder parents are worried."

"What about when stupid tabloid readers attacked a paediatrician?"

"That is entirely the fault of the politicians and the law-makers. People wouldn't need to take matters in to their own hands if the scum were locked up and properly medicated or preferably executed. Half the MPs in Parliament are morally suspect, so we can't rely on them to change anything."

"I'm wasting my time with you."

"You probably are if you expect me to go easy on perverts."

"Nazi."

"Oh that's it, very clever. If you can't argue the point, roll out the insults."

The man scowled and walked on as Fiona returned with a tray of croissants. "What was all that about?"

"Just the usual *Guardian*-reading ninny letting his heart bleed in public. Oh, 'pity the poor paedophiles'. What a poltroon, what an arse. I wonder if he'd be so understanding if some big swarthy 'victim of an uncaring society' sodomised his grandmother and left her for dead."

"Willie!"

He frowned and then smiled weakly as she placed his bacon and egg Panini and grande latte in front of him.

"Thanks," he grunted. "These people! I despise them, with their trendy pink blinkers, second-hand opinions and worthless degrees from the University of Smug...no doubt formerly the Polytechnic of Lingering Envy and Embittered Entitlement. After a while you can't even hear what they're saying, you can't distinguish the words. All you can hear is the soundtrack of a once-great civilisation sliding irreversibly into babbling madness."

Fiona shifted uneasily.

"Are we going to the reunion, dear?"

Broadwick groaned. An old classmate had been in touch, inviting them to what was threatening to become an annual get-together for four old school chums and their less than fragrant wives. They had been to grammar school together, but that was about all they had in common. None of his old friends had done as well as he had.

"Can't we say we've got a wedding to go to? Or a paint-drying display? I could say I'm going in for a hernia operation."

"Willie! They're your friends!"

"Correction, they *were* my friends."

"We should go."

"I'd rather watch a row of abandoned skips rust in the rain."

"Two hours tops. Just show your face. You've got enough enemies."

He grunted.

"Can I open the fan mail?"

"Be my guest."

Broadwick read his paper moodily as Fiona sorted the opened mail into piles – autograph requests, questions that required an answer, column suggestions and letters she felt might lift his mood. She resented it when people were mean to Willie, it was hard enough to get him out of the house at the best of times and she'd hate it if their Sunday brunches became even rarer. There were emails too, which she'd printed out and separated into similar precise piles.

"Oh here's a good one," she said. "From a farmer in Kent."

Broadwick grunted.

"He's congratulating you on your latest column. He says 'those who prey on the weak or the innocent should forfeit their right to live'."

"Good, good."

"Then he starts banging on about 'pikies'. Odd name. Gulliver Stevens, says he's a lay preacher. And this one is from an old dear who enjoyed you on Question Time and wants you to write about anti-English racism…Edie Piller, 73…"

"Humph. Let me have the farmer's letter, will you."

A passing van honked its horn and a driver gave him the thumbs up. "Good on yer Willie," he shouted. "Attaboy! Keep sticking it to the reds."

8

Bolton, Greater Manchester. Three hours later.

The landlady of the Oak had a face like her Mulberry handbag: tanned, sagging and leathery, but obviously pricey and generally open. Today she was looking a bit on the glum side, though.

"Don't worry Ivy, you might have your dates wrong," I said with a wink.

"By a decade, love," she said in an accent that could have been scraped straight off the walls of the Rovers Return and served up in one of Betty Turpin's hotpots. "Me ovaries shut up shop years ago."

"Woah. Way too much information, darlin'."

I'd gone in there for Sunday lunch, or dinner as proper people still called it. A decent all you can eat roast beef carvery, or at least all you can balance on your plate. I didn't mind the clientele, mostly Man City match boys mixed with some of life's older malcontents, and the odd wannabe WAG with Disney Princess hair, that now bog-standard Satsuma glow, false eye-lashes and full-on make-up. There must have been battles fought in less time than it takes the silly tarts to get ready to pop out for a Sunday drink.

"Fancy meeting you here!"

A woman's voice, a hand on my shoulder; I looked round apprehensively. Knockers!

"It's my hero," she continued.

"Ah, yeah. Katie, right. Katie from the kebab shop."

"You remembered."

She was pretty hard to forget. As well as the obvious, she was cute. 5ft 6, blue eyes, good legs, a low-cut white Kimono cotton top to show the wobble that meant real breasts, not stone-hard implants. The girl scrubbed up well, and the crowded Pandora bracelet on her right wrist said someone loved her. Better perfume today, too, Thierry Mugler Angel. I didn't like coincidences, though.

"What brings you around here?"

"Me Dad and step-mum live round the corner, but she's having a cow today so I thought I'd give them an hour or so to cool off. What are you drinking, chuck?"

"I'm fine, thanks."

"Come on, what kind of world would it be if a girl couldn't reward her knight in shining armour with a pint? Greene King is it?"

"Lager top as it's a Sunday. Thanks."

"Up here, that's a cocktail."

I laughed. We settled on a corner table. Katie ate olives and, uninvited, told me about her job in the bank and her life and how she'd broken up with her boyfriend after five years. I suffered in silence, while my eyes roved the pub and I calculated an escape route.

"So what about you?" she said finally.

"Not for me, thanks. I'm strictly a pork scratchings kind of guy."

"No. What do you do?"

"Oh, this and that. I got a job with the Samaritans last week, tried to phone in sick this morning but the bastards talked me out of it."

"Seriously!" she protested.

"Seriously? This and that. Bits and bobs."

"Ducking and diving?"

"Are you with the Inland Revenue?"

"NO!"

"OK. Anything considered as long as it's cash in hand. No income tax, no VAT. I don't take from society so I don't put anything back in the pot."

"That seems a bit anti-social."

"Not really. The whole system a con. Slaving your life away to pay for Lord Irvine's wallpaper? No thanks."

"My Dad would probably agree with you."

"Besides, I had to leave my last job through illness."

"Really?"

"Yeah. The boss got sick of me."

"Ouch! That hurt, but I'll let you off. I came here because I wanted to thank you. You were so brave with that druggie."

"Him? Junkies are nothing to worry about. The real nutters are the ones on steroids and anti-depressants."

"Interesting theory. Do you fancy eating, Harry, there's a decent gastro pub down the road, better than here?"

In my mind gastro wasn't a word that should be associated with pubs, just enteritis. But I lied politely.

"Look, I'm not being rude, I was going to go home, have a sarnie and watch the match." I drained my pint.

"Chelsea vs Bolton Wanderers?"

"Yeah."

"Oh can I come? I'm as Bolton as Dave Sutton's barnet."

I hesitated. The wobbling wonders were weakening my resistance.

"The place is a tip," I said finally.

"I know how men live, I've got brothers. What was it Rita Rudner said? 'Men are like bears with furniture'."

"But..."

"You sure you haven't got a wife tucked away at home? I wouldn't mind, it's not like you've tried it on or anything."

"I've got one ex wife who hates me and another one who's dead."

"I'm sorry."

"Don't be. It's not your fault."

She squeezed my hand. She was kind-hearted. And funny. More importantly, she was on the level. Not a threat.

"OK," I said. "But look, I'm warning you, it's a proper shit-hole."

"Is that accent Essex?"

"Kent," I lied. "At least that's what people shout at me in the street."

She got the gag after a beat and laughed. Her smile was wide and warm. Sexy. We never saw the match.

9

Surrey. An hour later.

Jackie Sutton sat astride the horse Daddy had bought her for her 21st birthday, and circled the paddock once again for effect. She sat up straight in the saddle, aware that her ample charms bounced with the horse's every step and that the stable owner's teenage son and his friends couldn't take their eyes off them.

Ever since she was a child, Jackie had been able to wrap men around her little finger with her smile. At fifteen, *der grossen Busen* appeared and the smile became almost superfluous. The legs, the arse...physically she was perfect. The only thing that spoilt the package was that she knew it. Jackie had been spoilt rotten by her investment banker father, and her uncles, and her lovers, and the big-wigs at Conservative Party HQ. Everything she got, she wanted. And now she wanted William Broadwick.

He wasn't the most handsome man she'd ever been to bed with, nor the best endowed – no mighty oak would ever grow from the Broadwick acorn. He wasn't even the best lover. But he had something Daddy's money couldn't buy: fame. Well, OK, infamy. The two were interchangeable these days. Broadwick's stringent views had rewarded him with celebrity status, and Jackie wanted some of that – which meant that she had to wrest Willie away from wifey. Surely not a problem for a woman of her connections, beauty and persuasive powers?

Jackie glanced over. The lads were still watching her. She circled again and rose in the saddle so they got a good look at her Pippa-perfect posterior before horse and rider left the paddock. Sweet dreams, boys, she thought. And make them wet ones.

10

Monday October 8th. Tunbridge Wells. 11am

Mick Neale had never said much, but these days he said even less. He was used to death – he'd been a soldier and he'd been a cop – but finding Tim Brown's corpse had given him nightmares. Thelma's body had been the only one he'd been hoping to see that weekend.

On the days when he didn't have his son, Mick would gravitate to the Toad Rock Retreat in Denny Bottom, which meant passing the murder scene. It made him shudder. Still, the first sip of Glenfiddich single-malt helped ease the pain. Something, some old cop instinct, intrigued him about the death. Not that the scumbag didn't deserve to die. Interfere with kids and you should forfeit your right to life. But this wasn't a crime of passion, and it certainly wasn't accidental. Brown had been deliberately, ruthlessly assassinated. Gunned down. Rubbed out. Blown away...whatever way you said it, it was disturbing.

It suddenly struck him that, in a cruelly ironic twist of fate, Toad Rock was in Harmony Lane...

Thelma wasn't on today, Len the landlord was behind the jump.

Mick ordered a fry-up.

"Two sausages, three rashers, two fried eggs and two toast..."

"That's bad for your heart, Mick."

"Yeah? Okay, make it three bangers, a fried slice and as much bacon as Lynn can fit on the plate. Hold the Holy Ghost."

"More people commit suicide with a fork than a gun."

"Fuck me, Leonard, who's boiled your piss today?"

Len nearly grinned. "It's being so cheerful as keeps me going," he said, as he took the order through to the kitchen.

"Terrible business, this," he said as he returned carrying a bottle of tomato sauce. "We had some DI in here today asking question. Gary Shaw. Know him?"

"Nope."

"Londoner. He said he'd heard of you."

"Yeah?"

"Did the Stevens girl know that other fella who got shot in Essex the same day, the one they're calling Donkey Don in the papers?"

"Donkey Don!"

"Because he did animal porn, not cos he was hung like one. Did the Stevens girl know him?"

"Charlie? Don't think so, why?"

"Only our Alice thought she'd seen them together at a bar in Brentwood the night before."

"Can't see it, she'd have said. It's not every day someone you know gets topped."

"I'll say."

"And what would she have been doing in Essex? The old fella doesn't like her drinking in the Pantiles, let alone over the water."

Mick did manual labour on a couple of local farms, including the Stevens one, so he knew the spiky curmudgeon about as well as anyone. The old man had a face like a depressed bloodhound and made the ancient *Up Pompeii* soothsayer seem like one of life's eternal optimists. Mind you, those bat ears of his would make anyone grumpy.

"It's amazing she's turned out so normal with the old man such an emotional cripple."

"Blimey Len, you need to knock *Loose Women* on the head."

"Ha. How is the old bastard, Mick? I saw him in town and he seemed a bit...disorientated. He told me the same story twice."

"Crankier than usual. He found a couple of pikies in the yard the other morning and fired off the 12-bore."

"He wants to watch that. The cops would sooner bang him up for defending his property than take on the gyppoes."

"That's what I told him, but he's spitting mad. They get away with murder."

"Different in your day, Michael."

"Everything was different in my day."

"Someone ought to teach them vermin a lesson."

11

October 9th. Bolton, Greater Manchester. 3am.

When I got tired of lying in bed watching Katie's breasts heave, I got up to pour myself a G&T. You'll be as pleased as I was to know that my initial impressions were bang on – they were all real and quite magnificent. Too many modern birds have bought into the fashion world *lie* that men go for a woman who looks like a thirteen-year-old boy in a training bra. Not so. Men who work in fashion go for that, but that is because they are largely pederasts. To men of my age and orientation, fake boobs are a cruel deception, a malicious con trick, like me strapping a king size cucumber down me pants. Not that I'd need to, I should add.

Katie got up minutes later to join me, wearing one of my Longshanks shirts.

"You're right, this place is a tip," she said, eyeing the boxes of stock in the living room like a disappointed school teacher.

"I did warn you. Red?"

"Go on then, just a small one."

I'd bought her a decent Fleurie instead of the £6 bottle of Bulgarian migraine she'd attempted to pick up in the offie.

"So what's your story, Harry?"

Where could I start? My real story would have made her hair curl. I'd been an undercover cop for years, one of the best thief-takers the Met had ever seen. Harry Tyler was the name I used to infiltrate gangs. My real one was Harry Dean, and my best and biggest job was the taking down of a South London firm led by Johnny Baker, known as Johnny Too – as in 'too handsome' – but Johnny Too Bad, like The Slickers song says, or too smart would have worked just as well.

"How d'you mean? I told you, I'm a trader."

She looked at the pictures on the wall of my two kids, Courtney Rose and little Alfie, named after Sir Alf Ramsay of course, a good Dagenham boy as well as being a bona fide football legend.

"Tell me about your wives."

It's a TV cliché that all detectives have their demons: the booze, the dead missus or the reckless infidelity. I had all three. I was married twice, but in reality, like all your favourite telly tecs, I was only really married to the job...until the job divorced me. My police career went tits up when I wiped out the Nelson brothers, the men who had driven my first wife, Dawn to suicide. MI5 set me up to be wiped out by the Provos in Dunleary, County Dublin, and if it hadn't been for a Prod paramilitary it would have been Goodnight Vienna. Dear old Tommy. His network had got me back onto the mainland and into a safe-house in North Wales. But there's only so much "No surrender" a boy from Colchester can take.

Do I feel bitter, hurt, isolated and betrayed? Yeah, for about a minute every morning, then I eat me black pudding and get on with things. Life sucks, wear a seat-belt.

I've been on me Jack for eight years now, living on my wits as a trader in black market goods up here in *Phoenix Nights* country. But what could I tell her? Dawn went over the side because I'm a nutter who can't do a 9-5 job. Kara left me for the same reason. And I don't see Courtney or Alfie for the simple reason that everyone who ever knew me – family, friends, former colleagues – thinks I'm dead; everyone except a couple of UDA boys, and no doubt British Military Intelligence.

I had hangovers every day but they weren't from drink, they were from memories.

No one to blame but me though... I was living proof that when it came to those closest to them, a good cop could also be a pretty lousy person.

"How about you," I asked out of politeness. "Anyone special?"

"There was one boy..."

"The one you told me about?"

"Yeah, the love of my life. But that's all gone down the plughole. I'm free, Harry, free but I'm not cheap." She smiled. "And if I seem to be channelling me dialogue from day-time soap operas, it's your fault for plying me with wine."

I took that as a cue to get up and pour more drinks, and came back to find her looking through my small CD collection – I'm old-fashioned like that, I like things I can actually possess rather than theoretically own in cyber-space. The extent of my modern music collection was a measly four CDs: Missing Andy, Buster Shuffle, Green Day and the Stone Foundation. The rest was strictly retro: The Jam, Madness, Squeeze, the Cockney Rejects, The Beat, a bit of Oasis. My last bird swiped all the Leela James.

Katie was examining All Mod Cons. "Before my time," she said, like that was any excuse. "Although my Dad was a Mod, into Northern Soul..." She found the Missing Andy CD. "Oh I like these, I saw these on Sky."

She looked at the discarded copy of the *Telegraph*, open on the Announcements page, and then the books on the side caught her attention.

"Do you read much, Katie?"

"Yeah, I'm just reading *Energy Secrets* by Alla Svirinskaya. She's an amazing healer and teaches you the secret of energy in the workplace and at home."

I did my best to hide my revulsion. "Dad's got this," she said, picking up a paperback edition of *Littlejohn's Britain*. "I said you'd get on. He supports the EDL."

I grunted.

"Y'know, English Defence League. What about you?"

"I'm more EDF."

"EDF? What's that?"

"Like the EDL, but more...electric, more energy in the home." She might laugh at that later, if she bothered to Google it.

"Are you teasing me?"

"Never!"

Katie leaned forward, smiled coquettishly and pushed her breasts up and out in my direction.

"Tit wank?" she asked innocently. Well what do you think? I was always taught it was rude to refuse a lady.

12

October 10. Tonbridge, Kent. 9.30am

DI Shaw walked into the incident room to find Detective Sgt Wattsie Watts sipping his coffee while she and DC Woodward finished off his favourite crossword.

"For fuck's sake, Rhona, I haven't read even that paper."

"You've not missed much, guv."

"Tart. Get the lads in will you?"

The briefing was quick and depressing. There were no new leads on the Brown killing, forensics had thrown up nothing other than the weapon was a Browning Maxus and there was still no clue as to the motive.

"Could it be a professional job?" Womble wondered aloud. "A hit-man, or a vigilante?"

"What? In Tunbridge Wells?" sighed Gary Shaw, "I can't see it, John. Five will get you ten that what we have here is a revenge shooting, so let's carry on checking out the whereabouts of the families of his victims and those close to them, and keep working through the list of his disgustingly creepy friends."

He drained the lukewarm dregs of his railway station crappuccino, and watched Womble concocting his morning glass of Fangocur, a revolting volcanic clay mix said to combat halitosis. Shaw cringed.

"Anything in my paper?"

"Justin Lee Collins found guilty," said Wattsie.

"Don't tell me, crimes against comedy?"

"Ta-da! You want your paper, guv? Only, I'd advise you to swerve Broadwick's Broadside on page eleven."

"What's that cock written now?"

13

Two hours earlier, Woking, Surrey.

William Broadwick beamed as his read his own column. This in itself was not unusual, but today's tour de force berating the national menace of 'travellers who never travel' tickled him more than normal. It was a comprehensive demolition job aimed at the 'tinker plague' and the wishy-washy liberal nitwits who 'seek to make them a protected species' and who 'would have us subsidise their feckless lifestyles indefinitely.' It rounded on the cops who 'fail to protect the honest citizens' and who 'allow camps of petty criminals to fester like a cankerous boil on what's left of our once grand way of life.' And then it worked up into a tub-thumping climax worthy of James Whale at his most populist. 'It is not racist to point out that gypsy camps go hand in hand with rising crime and spiralling mess. It is not racist to acknowledge that the growing subculture of tinkers, tarmac-layers and tax-dodging cheats and spongers is absurdly romanticised by urban intellectuals with absolutely no experience of the real world outside of their privileged enclaves. It is not racist to be moved to tears at the plight of innocent villagers who find their fields despoiled and their lives blighted by this cancerous plague.

'I do not suggest that all gypsies are dishonest,' he continued, building to a rousing climax. 'But we must address the problem of those who are, the worthless scum who flout the law and prey on their neighbours secure in the knowledge that their criminality will be protected by the 'uman rights brigade.

'They are not an endangered ethnic minority; they are not a romantic throw-back to a lost golden world. They are a plague of professional piss-takers with their heads in a trough of benefits provided by you and me and all the other poor mugs who actually work for a living, and if the courts and authorities refuse to deal with them, then we should not condemn anyone who does.'

Get in! Broadwick was so pleased with his words that he read them again. Take that, Littlejohn, he thought. I'm the Daddy now.

If William was happy at 7am, he was ecstatic by 10am, when the column was ranked at Number One on UK Twitter and Number Six worldwide. The Twitter storm continued to build throughout the day, with thousands of concerned bleeding heart tweeters – bleaters? – demanding that he be sacked from his job. But a poll privately commissioned by the *Express* showed that his views had a 91 per cent approval rating among their own readers, and equally strong support among those who identified themselves as regular *Daily Mail* readers.

Aware of her husband's rare good humour, Fiona asked again about the reunion and was pleasantly surprised when he said yes.

14

Eight hours later, Blackpool, Lancashire.

The setting sun was splitting slowly across the sky like a lap-dancer's legs at a brokers' stag do. Through the hotel net curtains I watched a seagull steal a chip from a toddler's hand. The birds up here were as brazen as the local conmen. I once watched a geezer selling seagulls by the South Pier for £20 a pop. He'd taken a couple's cash, pointed at a gull and said "Take that one." The dozy husband had only run along the beach trying to grab hold of it. Still, you can't spell gullible without gull...

I took a swig of ice cold Birra Moretti and smiled. Katie was in the shower singing Pink's 'Blow Me', which was ironic as just a few minutes ago my head had been stuck between her legs, the good old George Young going like clockwork on her clit. She certainly seemed to appreciate it – she'd gone from nought to hip bucking in about ninety seconds flat. Boris Johnson may have stormed the Tory conference today but I'd like to think that I went down better.

I'd come up here to get shot of 75 knocked-off Barbour jackets and a cotchell of porn DVDs, which was a dying game – the internet had killed that market stone dead. Some of the London boys were making more from recycling cast-off clobber to Eastern Europe than from Johnny Vaughan these days. But I didn't bother Katie with the business side. The jackets went in the car-park of the Viking while she was unpacking; the DVDs were in Jiffy bags down at reception for Kidder, an old mate to pick up later. I'd told her we were coming to the seaside for fish and chips. As it happened, I could still taste the fish, the chips would come at the casino after a couple of nice hours in La Fontana and a few bottles of Gavi di Gavi and no doubt I'd be reaching the vinegar about an hour after that. Nothing could possibly spoil a night like this.

I opened the wardrobe and laid out fresh schmutter for the evening. Smart casual I think; a simple black Hackett pullover, CK boxers, Levi red-tag jeans. No need for a whistle up here. And to round it off O'Keefe leather brogues – I love me trainers but you can't go to a casino in Kegler supers.

Katie came out of the bathroom wearing just a towel and a smile, and pecked me on the cheek. "You know, I'd love you to meet me Dad," she said. Oh shit. Then she stepped away and dropped the towel, and I didn't give her old man another thought.

15

Thursday, October 11.

A day after publication, Broadwick's Broadside was front page news in five of Britain's national newspapers. Not only had he scandalised the chattering classes, he'd also managed to provoke violent protests outside the *Express*'s office in Lower Thames Street. Traveller numbers were swollen by students, anarchists, squatters, professional agitators and various Labour activists, including two members of the London Assembly. The London Travellers' Unit had already got on to the Press Complaints Commission to register their anger. Their plummy-voiced brief insisted that Broadwick's column was "abusive, probably racist and certainly likely to inflame prejudice." The solicitor, whose membership of the Socialist Workers Party was not mentioned by the BBC News, called on Lord Leveson to demand "stringent state regulation" of the press in his forthcoming report, to be enforced with £1million fines. While the Radio 4 comedian, Jocelyn Tardy, a crotchety IRA apologist, remarked that Broadwick should be "muzzled like a rogue Rottweiler" and "put down like any other dangerous animal would be."

It was tremendous news for William Broadwick, who found himself being whisked by a succession of luxury cars from the Radio 4 Today programme to ITV's *This Morning*, and then on to BBC2's *The Daily Politics*, by which time he'd already been booked for the next night's *Question Time* and a high profile interview for the *Independent on Sunday*.

16

Paddock Wood, Kent. Midnight

To the casual observer, it looked as if the man in the muddy Land Rover Freelander was waiting for something. The driver wore a flat cap, a heavy navy Barbour Morris utility jacket and a dark Sullen Burnt flannel shirt. They would have seen the figure sit immobile and in silence for the best part of hour, they would not have seen that the driver was cradling a Browning Maxus. It was quite a gun. Its Power Drive Gas System was designed to perform under harsh hunting conditions; the Maxus delivered 18 per cent less felt recoil than its predecessor, and 44 per cent less muzzle jump for more accurate follow-up shots which instantly translated into more birds in your bag, if birds were your prey. Tonight, though, pheasants were off the menu. Instead it was peasants for starters. The driver's intention was to put the wind-up the inhabitants of an illegal traveller camp which Tunbridge Wells Borough Council seemed powerless to deal with.

It was one of the largest unauthorised sites in Europe. Stinking rubbish was strewn in splitting bags around the gate leading to the neighbouring site that they had been evicted from, where the council had bulldozed the old plots exposing former landfill that had been capped in the 1990s. It had cost £8.5million to clear the lot of them 100 yards down the road and make the situation worse. Rats abounded, as did stomach complaints and impetigo. Something had to be done.

At 12.30am, when the last caravan light had finally gone out, the driver went into action and was pleased to find that the manufacturer's claims about the Maxus were correct. The Lightning Trigger probably was the finest fire control system most shooters would ever encounter in an auto-loading shotgun. With lock-times averaging .0052 seconds, it was around 25 per cent faster than the nearest competing autoloader, making every pull perfect.

No fortune teller had seen this coming. The three and a half minute rampage burst every tyre and shattered every caravan window in range – so much for lucky heather. There were no serious casualties.

Eyewitnesses reported seeing just what the driver had wanted them to see: a burly head-case in a flat cap and

Barbour wax jacket wearing olive green army surplus trousers and Doctor Marten boots going to town with a shotgun. Job done. Within minutes of the assault ending, the Press Association received a phone call from someone using a voice distorter, calling themselves "Cam O'Dolland of the English Liberation Front." The caller claimed responsibility and demanded that the Coalition Government take "immediate" action against "the lawless gypsy plague."

17

October 12. Blackpool, six hours later

I snapped awake at 06.30am as usual, fully alert. Katie was dead to the world, snoring softly beside me like a contented kitten. I swung my legs out of bed, did thirty press-ups in the bathroom, dressed and went for a run along the new prom. I was back by 7.15, and picked up the package of cash that Kidder had left at reception in exchange for the DVDs. They'd be on sale at the local CIU clubs by dinner time. Two pints of lager, a pickled egg and a copy of *Womb Raider IV* please...

I was showered, shaved, eating toast and reading the paper by the time Katie surfaced.

"Why do you get the piggin' *Daily Telegraph*?" she moaned, a monstrous hangover taking the shine off her normally cheerful disposition.

"'Good morning wonderful' would have been a better way to start."

"Good morning wonderful," she smiled. "Thank you for blessing my day."

"Do you funny old Northern people really use the word 'pigging' in everyday conversation? I thought that was just in ITV sitcoms and Cannon and Ball scripts."

"Do you Southern folk really say, 'Gor-blimey, guv'nor, up the apples and pears mate'?"

"Only when we've got a cloth cap to doff. I suppose you like the *Sport* up here, all that 'I gave birth to a fish finger and now my fanny's got freezer burn' malarkey."

"I like the *Mail*," she said, a little sulkily.

"Yeah? Well, it's a woman's paper, that's why it's so spiteful."

"Why do you always buy the frigging *Telegraph*?"

"Force of habit...and I like the Matt cartoons."

"You always look at the Announcements, are you waiting for someone posh to have your baby?"

"Nah. Pippa Middleton wanted me, but I'm holding out for Ella Windsor, a bit more class don'tcha know?"

"Pippa! What's the fuss about her arse anyway?"

"Beats me, people just need to...get a grip..." I mimed a couple of thrusts.

"Harry!"

SO10 often used coded messages in the *Telegraph* to communicate with officers who were deep undercover. So it genuinely was force of habit, mixed with curiosity that made me peruse the small print of Britain's last surviving broadsheet every day. But civilians didn't need to know any of that. I flipped back to the front page. The main story was all about the attack on the gypsy camp. MPs were calling for the English Liberation Front, which I hadn't even heard of, to be classified as a proscribed terrorist group.

"Are we going for breakfast or what?"

"What."

"I've got a throat like a junkie's carpet."

"Thank you Countess Violet, how on earth is Downton Abbey coping without you?"

She tweaked my left nipple. "Come on, I need me sausage."

Her hand slide slowly down my body until it reached its target.

"What's this?" she asked coquettishly. "Cumberland?"

"Horse meat."

"You wish! You are quite a handful though."

"I think I'm starting to rub off on you."

"Don't you dare waste it!"

"I meant my sense of humour."

"I know! Nowt wrong with that. And where better for a bit of seaside postcard filth than Blackpool?"

"I thought you'd come here to ride the Big One?"

"I did. And after that I'll get up and go t'Pleasure Beach." She gurgled like a happy child.

"My last wife used to say that being with me was like living in a *Carry On* film," I said. "In the good weeks..."

"That's crackin', I love the Carry Ons...except for *Carry On Behind*, before you ask."

"How else are you going to brown the sausage?"

"Urgh. You spooner."

"Northern slang, does not compute."

Her Blackberry buzzed. "It's Dad," she said, releasing her grip. "He's still okay to meet us on Saturday, but he's going on a demo first."

"What demo?"

"Supporting William Broadwick."

18

Tonbridge, Kent. 11.15am

DC Woodward had first remarked upon a possible link between the recent spate of murder and crime on their manor and the Broadwick column. Timothy Brown berated, Timothy Brown killed; gypsies berated, a camp shot up...

Woodward, known as Don because of his history degree, spelt out the theory hesitantly, adding "It could be coincidence..." But DI Shaw's instincts told him it was worth a shot. Don and Wattsie had gone online and diligently uncovered a string of similar links, ranging from the murder of Simon Loewy to more trivial crimes, all committed within days of a Broadwick column connection.

The first obvious one occurred in January 2012, when William had hit out at 'the greedy bankers who wrecked our economy', suggesting they were pirates who deserved to receive jail sentences rather than hefty bonuses. The next day, the manager of the RBS bank in Maidstone had been kidnapped, drugged, dressed up as a buccaneer and deposited outside of his own building in stocks next to a box of fresh eggs and a poster saying 'Robber Banker, Egg Me At Will', signed by one Miles Farger. All six eggs had been used with unnecessary enthusiasm in the ten minutes before he was liberated.

Other cases included a shock rock band called the Orgasm Guerrillas who had scandalised the authorities at the University of Kent by punching and kicking apig's head on stage before showering the student audience with fresh butchers' offal. Broadwick took the "infantile middle-aged rebels" to task, and, six days later, the band's next gig at the Dome in Tuffnell Park, North London, had five tons of pig shit deposited on the venue's doorstep. Locals joked that it had improved the smell.

In total, there were thirteen examples of possible Boardwick-inspired vigilante actions.

"If they are all related, he's gone from silly, almost surreal protests to serious crime," noted Womble. "Starting locally and moving out of the county..."

"Cam O'Dolland," added Wattsie thinking aloud. "Cameron is Scottish, O'Dolland sounds Irish...and he's saying he is English."

"Must have one of those multiple personalities," said Don.

"Or he's just a mixed-up fuck," grunted Gary Shaw.

"Here's the thing though, before 2012 Cam O'Dolland was a Googlewhack," Wattsie added.

"A what?" said Womble.

"Something that if you'd typed it in Google and hit search would result in absolutely nothing results being found," explained Don, as Wattsie absent-mindedly wrote the name down on her note-pad. "There is no Cam O'Dolland on police, revenue or NHS records either, which would suggest that either he's foreign or it's an alias. The only mention Rhona could find of an English Liberation Front was on a David Icke website – some chap called Gullick talking about starting a peaceful protest and an 'activists' group called the ELF focusing on, and I quote 'the destruction of our civil liberties and raising awareness about the London bombings'."

"Could be a nutter," replied Womble.

"What? On a David Icke website?" laughed Shaw. "Seems unlikely, Wom. Check out this Gullick character, please. Unlikely, but have a sniff around. This is good work though, guys. If there is a real link between William Broadwick's column and O'Dolland's statements, as there appears to be, then we can use it to flush out his groupie."

"So what will you do next, guv?" asked Wattsie.

"Speak to the boss," he replied. "I think I've got a plan."

19

Paddock Wood, Kent. Midday.

Gulliver Stevens sat at his desk trying to compose a letter to William Broadwick. He knew the word he wanted, it was on the tip of his tongue but it just wouldn't come. The desk was a cluttered mess of largely unopened bills. He picked up the imitation Mauser blade with SS markings that he used as a paperweight, and pulled it from its scabbard. He'd known exactly what he had wanted to say a moment ago, and now it had gone. He'd re-read the column, that was it, and then it would all come back to him. He took a sip of coffee from his mug and then realised it was not only cold but possibly a day or two old. At that moment he was also aware that he stunk. It was the same body odour he had smelt on his father and uncles back in the days before deodorants; an honest odour, redolent of hard work, but even so.

Where was the girl? The girl would put everything right. Where was she?

A noise in the yard disturbed him. He rushed out of the office, grabbing his shotgun from the kitchen and ran out of the back door to confront the intruder who was over by the barn in between the Land Rover and the old Ford Transit van.

"Who the fuck is that?" Gulliver shouted. "Put yer hands up you pikey bastard!"

Mick Neale took a step back and turned to face him. "It's me, Mr Stevens. It's Mick. I've come to do the chores."

"Mick?"

"Yes. Mick Neale. Look, you know me."

Mick stepped forward. The old farmer peered at him, his freakishly large ears accentuated by a severe haircut.

"Michael!" said Gulliver; his ruddy face lightened into a smile. "Good to see you, chum. Did I tell you we've had pikies robbing us? I saw off two of them the other day."

"Yes, you told me Mr Stevens."

"Lazy, thieving, gypsy bastards, preying on honest people. It's a bloody disgrace."

"That it is. I was going to clean out the barn for you. Where do you want the propane gas cylinders putting?"

Stevens looked blank. "Propane gas?" he repeated vaguely.

"Yes, there are a couple of cylinders in here, next to all the chemicals."

"Chemicals?"

"Yes you've got potassium chlorate in there, fertiliser, sulphur."

"Sulphur?"

"Are you okay, Mr Stevens? Gulliver?"

"Yes, yes. Did I tell you we've had pikies robbing us? I saw off two of them the other day."

A Honda Civic drove into the yard, parking between the transit van and Mick's old RAV4. The driver, a stunning brunette, got out, looking puzzled.

"Charlie!" said Mick with relief. "Thank God you're here, I think your Dad's having a funny turn."

She was wearing a smart, knee-length, Isabel de Pedro one-piece, business-like, but still incredibly sexy. She had dancer's legs, sturdy but sexy.

"Are you okay, Dad?" she said, putting her arm around the clearly befuddled farmer. "Let's get you inside, and run you a nice bath. Thanks Mick, I had to go into London for a business meeting. Dad's been a bit out of sorts lately. Nothing to worry about."

"What would you like me to do, sort out the small barn?"

"No," she said sharply, adding: "No, no thanks. I've got some of my cousin's stuff in there, nowhere else to put it really. But you would be doing me a huge favour if you could clear out the cellar. All the old tat that's in there can go in the small barn too, if that's okay. Probably only take you an hour. £30 cash in hand okay?"

"Lovely job. And Mr Stevens?"

"He'll be okay, he's just forgotten his medication again."

Mick watched her walk the old man indoors. Her lipstick was so vivid he could practically taste it. Stevens stopped by the back door and waved at him. "Cheerio Michael," he said loudly. "We'll go fly-fishing again soon, my boy."

"Pip pip, Mr Stevens."

Mick Neale shook his head. They had never gone fly-fishing together, ever. Poor old Gulliver. Mick decided that if the time ever came, he'd rather be whacked to death with a shovel than end up like this.

Mick followed them into the house and walked towards the cellar, wary of Myrtle, the farmer's malignant cat. He had first encountered the semi-feral Burmese the previous summer. It had been a swelteringly hot day and as Mick was working outside, he'd taken his shirt off. Myrtle had very kindly dropped onto his head from the barn roof and slid down his bare back with her claws extended. The scars were still visible. They'd had a hate-hate relationship ever since, with Myrtle generally coming out on top.

After he'd finished clearing the cellar, Mick took his envelope of cash from the kitchen table and drove over to the fields at the back of the cow-sheds, just to clear his head. He lit a roll-up and watched a weasel tease a much larger rat, running rings around the paralysed rodent until it finally sunk its teeth into the critter's neck. For a crazy moment Mick wondered if nature had been acting out a metaphor on his behalf, a metaphor so arcane that he couldn't quite decipher it.

20

Blackpool, Lancashire. 10pm.

I told her it was a mistake to go to a gay club, not because I don't like irons but because the music was shit, the compere was a Northern Premier League version of Lily Savage and it was a fucking trannie night. So the place was full of big geezers in drag, and I mean geezers. These were blokes so pig ugly they made Twisted Sister look like the Saturdays. We had one drink and did the offski, but were followed out to the car park by two men in frocks.

The older one was trying to seem menacing, which is difficult when you look like a fatter, butcher version of Les Dawson done up as his less than alluring Ada character. I wanted to laugh, but now probably wasn't the time. His big, morose face stretched into a smile that didn't look anything like genuine happiness. He spoke in a low, comically incongruous growl.

"Are you Harry?"

I nodded cautiously.

"Harry Tyler?"

"Yep."

"I'm John Finlay. I know an old friend of yours."

I knew the name and a shufti at his hands told me the rest. Sausage Fingers Finlay, a local heavy...probably not often seen in black nail varnish though.

"Oh yeah?"

The smile had gone. "Yeah, Douglas Richards."

Dougie The Dog!

Baring his teeth, Finlay came straight at me, brandishing a cosh. Katie screamed. Before he could swing it, I sent a shuddering right to his gut. The tool went flying. The big man roared and threw a wild left which I swerved, catching him off balance with the return punch. Another sharp right sent him straight to the floor. I got in a kick that knocked him sparko when his pal threw a left to the side of my jaw. It was a good one, I felt it. But it wasn't good enough. I spun round, fists up ready to take him too only to see Katie blast him square on with a Taser X26. Ho! Resourceful girl! Have it!

I grabbed her hand and we headed straight for the taxi rank in Talbot Road, about 200 yards away. We were in the sherbet and heading back to the South Pier before either of the two goons was fully conscious.

Katie spoke first. "I didn't fancy yours much."

"Ha. Talk about handbags at dawn. How long have you been packing a Taser then?"

"Since after the kebab shop incident."

"Well, thanks."

"One good turn deserves another."

We sat in silence for thirty seconds. "So come on then, action man," she said. "What was all that about? Explain."

I shrugged. "I didn't know either of them."

"Douglas Richards?"

"An arsehole from way back...sex-case. Loudmouth. Bully."

"How does this Finlay know you, then?"

"I really ain't got a clue."

She smiled. "The sins of the past cast a long shadow, Harry, as I'm sure you know. I'll tell you what though, petal. It sure as hell knocked spots off the cabaret."

"So you're not angry then?"

"Angry? No. More...turned on..."

Her hand found my thigh. Here we go! Some guys have all the luck.

21

Maidstone, Kent. Midnight.

William Broadwick sat on the hotel bed, head in his hands, groaning like a wounded bison. Jackie Sutton bent over and kissed his forehead gently. "It wasn't that bad, Willie. You did well, in the circumstances."

Ah, the weasel disclaimer. The circumstances being his righteous sentiments about the traveller problem had been sabotaged by the deranged gun-happy maniac going completely over the top. It was a miracle no one had died. Naturally this had made his *Question Time* appearance somewhat less of a triumph than he'd been hoping.

"You are not to blame for a random psychopath," Jackie went on, soothingly. "Judges and corrupt politicians are, for allowing the injustice to fester. Besides, you were lucky. The Labour Party guy tonight was as camp as Christmas, the 'fashionable comedy booking' wasn't remotely funny, the Lib-Dim woman was a waste of space and the Tory was as wet as fresh cement and just as grey. Most of the studio audience were on your side, and so would the viewers at home have been."

"Do you think?"

"I know, silly."

"I felt like a human spittoon, talk about shot by both sides. Dimbleby was a disgrace."

"Well, what else would you expect from Dimblebore? You handled yourself well, and that's what matters. Twitter is split 50/50 but a) we know that's top-heavy with envious leftie trolls and b) there is enough real drama out there tonight to bury the gypsies way down tomorrow's news lists."

"Like what?"

"Seven Royal Marines arrested, more on Savile, Andrew Mitchell, gas power stations..."

"Good, good."

"Listen to me. This is all great for your profile. You are becoming the voice of the common man – nobody in the real world gives a crap about what the Guardianistas think except other Guardianistas. You could be our generation's Enoch Powell – forthright and principled, the politician who speaks his mind and tells it like it is. You could be Boris without the bumbling, Farage with a real prospect of actually getting elected. We can get you a safe Tory seat, Willie. Trust me, this is just the beginning for you. When is the interview with the *Independent*?"

"Tomorrow, 12.30 at Rules."

"Nice. Now, listen I know I'm teaching my grandmother to suck eggs here – but remember, she will be as nice as pie to your face, but will be looking to trip you up at each and every pass. So you have to be aware of that, *at all times,* even when her tape recorder is off. I wouldn't put it past the bitch to have another one on the go out of sight somewhere. She'll want you to portray you as cold, posh and pompous. Your job is to be polite, warm and charming, to show your human side."

"So big up the missus."

"Absolutely, and the charity work. And it wouldn't hurt to mention that school reunion you told me about. That makes you seem down to earth, you're a big successful media star but you've still got time for the kids you went to school with, those lifelong friends in crappy old jobs."

"Yes, yes. I get that."

"You're a winner who has still got time for the losers...but don't say that, obviously."

"Of course not, but that's the conclusion people will draw."

"Exactly," she smiled. "And look what else you've won..."

She stepped back, and lifted her dress to display her garter belt and the tops of her cream silk stockings. Broadwick's smile turned into a leer. He stood up expectantly.

"Hold on, Romeo. Are you feeling thirsty? Want me to order room service champagne?"

"Yes," said Broadwick, suddenly brighter. "Better get two or three bottles and a few cold beers. This could be a long night."

On past experience, Jackie doubted it.

"Just let me come first, big boy," she said, adding the "for once" in her head.

22

Eleven Hours Later.

William Broadwick woke up with a jolt when the Estonian maid tried to get into the hotel room to clean it for the third time. His right hand was still strapped to the bedside table with his own belt. He had a vague memory of Jackie waking him before she left, and a head that felt like Thor had been using his brain for a lengthy session of thunder practice. Shit. He was supposed to be meeting the blasted woman from the *Independent On Sunday* in Rules in about 90 minutes' time. He'd never make it by train now. Shit, shit and double shit.

The mini-cab to Covent Garden set Broadwick back a painful £65, rounded up to £70. If that left him ratty, it was nothing to the look of exasperated irritation on the face of legendary feature writer Nell Butcher when he finally arrived 35 minutes late. William turned on the charm, apologising profusely, blaming a burst water main at New Cross and generously buying his interviewer a bottle of the dearest claret on the menu all for herself. He stuck to London Pride, as he was pretty sure he was still over the limit from last night.

Butcher, known as the hatchet woman of Fleet Street and more memorably 'the velociraptor with mascara', visibly cheered as she rattled through the bottle of Bordeaux's finest. She had the mutton broth and grilled Dover Sole, he went for the man of the people option – battered haddock with chips and mushy peas.

The conversation was sparky to begin with. Butcher pulled no punches as she hit him with rumours and smears, even trotting out what Broadwick called "the old canard" of him being tapped up to run as a candidate for the British National Party – it was entirely true but the one-to-one meeting with a senior party official had been entirely private, so there was no way for any journalist to stand it up. William laughed it all off, even the whispers that he'd once shared a mistress with London Mayor Boris Johnson.

"Who'd want BoJo's sloppy seconds?" he'd asked. "I'm far too old for a Boris Bike! Can you imagine the big oaf frolicking between the sheets like a wet otter? No thank you. No, no, no.

"Seriously, Nell," he went on with a disarming smile. "I've stopped reading about myself on the internet. I've had to! It's like the wilder realms of science fiction out there. If you believe Wikipedia, I played rugby for the All-Blacks and have three nipples and a Prince Albert piercing. No, I was a Marxist at 15 but I've been a Tory all my adult life, and I'm not apologetic about it. It's like Denis Healey said, 'If you're not a Commie at eighteen you have no heart, and if you're still one at 30, you have no blinking brain."

Nell visibly relaxed as she demolished her second bottle of claret. She had a hard, unfeminine face, more lived-in than a Camden squat, but the laughter lines hinted at the softer, more-rounded person behind the ferocious public image. The conversation turned to the journey, and Broadwick made the old trout laugh out loud with his account of being driven through Peckham "watching the late morning ASBO yobs sharing fags and spliffs and cans of strong breakfast lager while listening to crap-rap on no doubt stolen iPods..."

"And the boys were just as bad," interjected Nell.

He laughed enthusiastically. "Touché! The girls, though! Let me tell you about the girls. Half of them are pushing prams, all of them are chewing gum as vacantly as cows chewing cud, all of them are showing off their midriffs – in this weather! I haven't seen that many piercings this side of a hospital ward in a war zone."

"And who do you blame?"

"New Labour! The welfare system! Dozy parents! Trendy teachers! Lax schools! The permissive society! Agony aunts! The BBC! MTV and its deluge of culture-wrecking filth! Most of these girls should be at bloody school. They are sixteen, fifteen;, maybe fourteen. They've been caked in make-up since they were eight and sexually active since before they had pubic hair. They know nothing, do nothing and aspire to nothing, a lost generation sacrificed on the altar of progressive education and the socialist hatred of self-improvement and aspiration."

She smiled wryly. "You really are the *Express*'s 'Call Me Old-Fashioned...' columnist, aren't you?"

"Well, yes and no. It's true that you won't be catching me dancing to 'Gangnam Style' any time soon, or bopping away at a One Direction concert but I'm not exactly advocating a return to feudalism."

Nell gave a throaty, whisky laugh. "But you are a dyed in the wool old time hang-'em and flog-'em Conservative."

"I am, and very proudly so – which is why I dislike the political Titanic we call the Coalition, why I abhor the EU and why I don't need to lie about the last time I ate a Cornish pasty. I'm certainly not in favour of 80 pence in the pound taxation or squeezing successful businessmen until they've all fled the country. I don't want to drive us back to the bad old Britain of the late 70s like some of your readers would like to do, but I'd settle for the tax-cutting free market days of Maggie's booming Britain."

Butcher decided to swerve a tedious full-on Thatcher debate and instead got him to open up about Fiona, their pain at being childless, their home lives, and their friends. Broadwick mentioned the reunion – with his "dear dear pals from school, we've kept in touch for more than thirty years."

"What do they do?" she asked, almost catching him on the hop.

"Let's see. Mark is a teacher, Peter is a civil servant, Chris is a builder, Paul, ah, well until recently Paul worked in an office at BBC TV Centrebut, please don't print this, he had a nervous breakdown quite recently and I'm not sure if he's back at work."

"So none of them have done as well as you?"

"No," he agreed too readily, but recovered by quickly throwing in "but so what? They're as happy with their career achievements as I am with mine." He changed the subject, niftily he felt, to a joke his friend Paul had told him about the BBC having a rowing contest with a Japanese TV company back in the Nineties, which the Corporation had lost.

"John Birt set up a working party to try and find out why," he said. "They found that while the Japanese had eight people who were rowing and one steering, the BBC team had one rowing and eight steering. The working party decided to employ consultants to come up with a solution. They decided that the BBC needed three steering managers, three deputy steering managers and a director of steering services. The rower, meanwhile, should be made to row harder. When they took on the Japs and lost again, the director of steering services decided to sack the rower, sell the boat and give himself a pay rise."

There were tears of laughter rolling down the hatchet face of the hatchet woman of Fleet Street. William beamed. They ordered sticky toffee pudding and a cheese board and he told her outrageous off the record stories about the Editor's temper, the feature editor's string of married lovers, the explosive and quite unprintable identity of Cameron's former communication director's seven year bit on the side, and how violent the Picture Editor got in drink, which happened pretty much any day with a 'D' in its name. The interview had turned into a classic hack bitch fest, which was far more fun, and after they'd drained their brandies they tottered around admiring the pictures that covered every square inch of wall before bursting out onto Maiden Lane, hugging like reunited lovers, and sailing off in taxis.

It had all gone very well.

23

Saturday October 13. Worsley, Greater Manchester. 8.45pm.

We arrived at the hotel late to discover that, like the patches of paint around the window ledges, the charm of the once-grand Victorian inn had long since faded. Any appeal it might once have possessed had peeled away at the edges, along with any vestige of class.

In the large function room, the meeting had already started. An over-weight geezer with greased-back grey hair and elaborate Rhodes Boyson side-burns was addressing a room full of around forty people, a mix of young heavies, middle-aged men in charity shop suits and disgruntled pensioners.

"That's Dad," whispered Knockers indicating the speaker.

I nodded. Dad – Kenneth McManus – wore a grey three-piece pin-striped whistle with a flash pink breast pocket handkerchief. He was only a pencil moustache short of a sitcom spiv. It wouldn't have surprised me too much if he'd opened up his jacket to reveal a set of watches for sale stitched into the lining, or if he had started selling black market beef from his briefcase.

Dad was standing in front of a banner that declared 'Defend Free Speech'. On both ends were posters with the same hand-written felt-tip pen slogan: 'I'm Backing Broadwick'. He was speaking passionately about the threat to the "British way of life" posed by gypsies and Islamists. Mention of either word provoked a murmur of approval and occasionally light applause.

I tuned in to that voice. It sounded Salford to me. He was talking about "Romanian gypsies", saying "We are importing the scum of Europe – pickpockets, thieves and beggars; experts at helping themselves to your watch and wallet or a nice few grand of undeserved benefits, thank you very much. And thousands more will pour into this country in January 2014, when 29 million people from Romania and Bulgaria gain the right to live and work unrestricted in Britain under European 'freedom of movement' rules that we don't have a say in."

There were shouts of "No!" and "Never." 'Dad' was playing the crowd like a Stradivarius. Something nagged me about him, though, apart from the dress sense and saloon bar rhetoric. I'd seen this bloke before. I recognised the smirk. He was one of those jerks, those shifty cowboy berks who lurk in the murk where no one looks, where the Old Bill sniff around but can't quite shine a torch.

Katie obviously believed her father was another struggling small businessman with a few harmless Arthur Daley tendencies, but my Spidey senses were tingling. When I'd first seen him, he was definitely a Kim Jong-un – a wrong'un. Under the radar, like me, but rotten with it...

On he went, attacking Irish tinkers "the tarmac mafia, the big fat gypsy tax-dodgers."They weren't "the proper Romany gypsies," he said. "Not like the benign old folk you see on Blackpool pier and at race tracks; cross their palm with silver and they'll tell you a lie..."

That was it! Race tracks. It all fell into place. I'd seen him at Aintree a few years ago, with Andrew Palmer, a heavy from Fleetwood known as Pancake, and a big-time Scouse drug baron called Nutty Butty, short for Nigel 'Nutty' Butterfield. It was obvious they knew each other well. It was a sure bet that dear old Dad was laundering Butty boy's filthy lucre, or processing some other dirty deal, through his chain of backstreet garages, market stalls and the garment factory Katie had often mentioned.

The crowd were perking up. Dad was working up to his big finish and they knew it.

"Everywhere we look, our British way of life is under attack. Our freedom of speech is undermined by liberal judges. Our laws are sabotaged by the European Court of 'Ooman Rights. Our values – the values our ancestors fought and died for – are being pissed away by Muslims, sorry 'Islamists', and their bleeding heart pinko apologists. Will we allow this to carry on?"

"NO!" responded the crowd.

"No, we will not," Dad continued. "We cannot. There is a new Battle of Britain brewing, folks. It's not a hot war, an open war or an honest war, it's a stealth war, a concerted assault on British values, our freedoms and our civil liberties, hard-worn over the centuries. Men like William Broadwick are targeted by the people who hate this country – the wets, the reds and the PC rats – because they tell the truth. If you want to help the fight back, then back Broadwick, and please, I beg you, throw a fiver or any loose change you can spare into the buckets that are coming round now. With your help, and William's, God willing, we shall take our country back."

The room erupted. The crowd stood and cheered – and as they did, two men in Stone Island navy blue blouson jackets left their chairs a few feet from me and started making towards the front. I noticed the glint of metal in the front runner's hand. Matey boy had a Stanley knife.

Quickly, I grabbed one of their deserted chairs, chased after them and crowned them both with one good hard swing. The blade fell to the floor a few feet from Dad. I drew some puzzled looks but Knockers was on hand quickly to join the dots. Suddenly, I was a hero.

Their wallets told a story. The younger one, Tim Brennan was 22, and the proud owner of an expired NUS card; the would-be blades man Al Lynch was 31 and signing on. The stewards dragged the pair of them into a cleaner's cupboard and waited on the cops. I, in turn, was dragged to the bar by Katie's Dad and a merry throng of blokes his age.

I sipped one of the three pints of Cascade that had been lined up for me already, with another two in the pipe. They had pints and chasers.

"Does that happen often?" I asked.

"The Reds? Aye," Ken replied. "Too often, and when they haven't got the numbers they've got the tools."

I grunted. "I'm not saying that I agree with everything you said tonight," I said. "But I do know I support your right to say it, just like I'd support their right to protest against it. But you can't have people getting carved up for having an opinion. This isn't fuckin' a 1920s bierkeller, it's not Moscow. We used to have a thing in this country called free speech, and once we lose that, we lose the cornerstone of everything that matters."

"Hear, hear," cried half a dozen beered-up blokes.

"I mean, they call you fascists, but that really is fascism, isn't it? Trying to maim and kill people because you disagree with them."

Ken slung his arm around me. "We'll have you making speeches for us yet, Harry lad."

"Is this the City boy your Katie's sweet on?" asked a chubby, red-faced man called Gregg.

"City boy?" I said indignantly. "I do a bit of trading, mate, I ain't won the *Apprentice*."

"Ooh 'eck, I love his accent," purred Gloria, the landlady, who for some unknown reason was wearing a Stetson and occasionally drinking vodka shots out of a water pistol.

She seemed a nice, friendly woman but I couldn't help but notice that her entire sun-leathered boat-race was the colour of Kia-Ora, which was a little disconcerting to say the least. It wouldn't be too unkind to observe that she looked a lot better from the other side of the room.

Gloria's Botox-frozen forehead said forty, the saggy old Deirdre Barlow Gregory added another twenty-five years. The bust looked positively fortified. If she took off her bra she wouldn't need socks.

"He could be in *EastEnders*, couldn't he lads?" She winked lasciviously, and my testicles involuntarily retreated up into the safety of my body.

Don't get me wrong, I'm not a misogynist, I like women. I just don't want to shag a great-Gran, you know what I mean? Not outside of a desert island with no hope of escape. I'm not Wayne Rooney.

I smiled at her politely and turned back to my Cascade.

"He is a right diamond geezer," said Ken in his best Cockney accent, which sounded painfully Australian to my Britneys.

"'Ere, who is the most knackered man in Walford?" asked Gregg. "The poor bastard who dug Heather Trott's grave."

The landlady laughed and waltzed away to serve a party at the other end of the bar. Her hem was practically skimming her vulva. She was mutton dressed as an ultra-sound scan of lamb foetus.

"You see that?" Ken whispered to me conspiratorially. "I had that in every hole last week. Cracking fuck. Nipples like Eartha Kitt's face."

This was an image that even shut me up. "Cool," was the only word I managed to get out, although the phrase that sprang to mind was "Get a tomb." I felt like I'd wandered into the Twilight Zone.

"Ignore them," said an elderly white-haired man, who introduced himself as "Albert, Albie Simmons", adding "They're all soppy in drink."

Gloria looked over and winked again, more lasciviously this time.

"Would you call her a cougar, Kenneth?" asked Gregg. "Or maybe a sabre-tooth? Fanny like the Mariana Trench, I shouldn't wonder."

"Now, now. Nothing wrong with an older woman with a healthy sex drive," Ken protested. "As long as you replace the petroleum jelly with Polygrip Ultra."

Frank, a saggy, pale-faced man who looked like a 300-year-old turtle in a golf jumper spoke for the first time."Is it vajazzled down there, Ken, or just stone-clad?"

Gregg chuckled. "Good luck Kenneth I say. They do reckon sex is the best form of exercise, although I can't see two minutes a month getting shot of this beauty."

He lifted his shirt and flashed a gut like an over-inflated Space Hopper. "And it all turns to cock after midnight!"

The party exploded in hearty laughter, except for old Albert who tutted under his breath. "I'd best be making a move," he said. He pulled me closer and said quietly. "Don't think badly of them. They hit the brandies after the attack. You can't blame them."

"I've heard worse," I smiled and then glanced around for Knockers.

"Don't worry about the women," said Ken. "Katie is over there with my Liz. They're happy as Larry. Right, who's got a gag for me?"

"I'll start you off," said Gregg. "And this is true by the way – I'm going to take part in the Great Bradford Run next Sunday. It's not an official race, I just stand in the city centre & shout 'Allah is a tosser' and then off we go..."

"Bradford," groaned Ken. "I went there once and felt like a spot on a domino. I called 999 and got the Bengal Lancers."

"What does Bonanza mean in Spanish?" asked Chris, a small man from Clitheroe with a face like a beetroot in distress.

"I give up," said Ken.

"Who set fire to the map!"

"Why did Scargill wear a baseball cap?" chimed in Gregg. "Cos he knew it would be...three strikes and out."

I groaned inwardly. Bonanza, Scargill and Bernard Manning gags...it was hardly *Mock The Week* was it? What next, jokes about Harold Macmillan and rationing, or *Dixon Of Dock Green*? Heard the one about Alma Cogan? They were all too sloshed for a proper chinwag.

"I saw in the paper that Greater Manchester police are looking for a Mosque arsonist," contributed Frank. "I phoned the information line and sadly it wasn't a job advertisement."

"Ha. Nice one," I said, managing half a grin. "'Scuse me, lads, just nipping off to point Percy at the porcelain."

"Very Australian of you," observed Gregg. "Go on, Harry lad, go unbutton the mutton."

As soon as I'd locked the cubicle door I was on the phone to Knockers. "Time to make a move Katie," I said. "You look so ravishing tonight I can't keep my hands off ya for a moment longer."

It took ten minutes for her to say her goodbyes. Ken and Liz had gone outside for a fag. As we drove off, I saw him slap her in the rear-view mirror. Another reason not to like the cunt.

***

Later that night I lay in bed mulling it all over. Ken McManus was definitely not for me. Granted, he had a point about a few things and several people at the meeting were probably well-meaning and sincere, but there was much more to Ken than met the eye. If he was involved, there had to be pound notes in this and possibly something else, something much more poisonous disguised as common sense to slip past your defences. It was likely to be the political equivalent of someone splintering shards of glass into dough and then baking you up the kind of cake that kills you from the inside.

23

Sunday, October 14.

Nell Butcher had lived up to her reputation. *Private Eye* wit Francis Wheen would dub her William Broadwick profile in the *Independent On Sunday* "the greatest demolition job since they blew up the Stardust Resort and Casino in Las Vegas." It was a merciless onslaught, describing the columnist as 'a bubbling pool of sulphurous mud, fulminating mindlessly against a changing world that is leaving him behind.' The opening words were: *'Want to know what William Broadwick hates? Pretty much everything. From the moment his front door shuts behind his lardy posterior, poor William is in enemy terrain, darting and diving into cabs, restaurants and private clubs to avoid the awful heaving masses of humanity littering the path with their stupidity, their everyday banalities and their "all-consuming" lowbrow culture. He hates the poor, their children, the disadvantaged, the working class, the underclass, teachers and the Labour Party...and that's before he gets started on travellers.'*

Broadwick, she claimed, had invited her to Rules because it was *'one of the few places he fitted in; a mouldy old mausoleum with its walls lined with two dimensional caricatures and portraits of dead moustachioed bores...the sort of men who would have laughed as they had slaughtered the unfortunate deer whose once proud antlers are triumphantly displayed among the hunting prints, statuettes, busts, stained glass and dull architectural drawings.'* He is, she wrote, *'an obstreperous ghost of times past and values either gone or nearly forgotten, spewing out goblets of prejudice and saloon bar hatred; a dying echo of imperial delirium.'*

For all of the columnist's combative infamy, he was *'one of life's bores...,'* she said, asserting that *'women terrify him. I ask about previous girlfriends, one night stands, flirtations and infidelity, he breaks into a sweat. The very notion of sex seems to terrify him, especially unorthodox sex; homosexuality disgusts him as much as it seems to fascinate him...his hate list includes most foreigners, modern art, modern comedians, modern pop, modern television, lads' mags (which he calls "pornography for cretins"), rich leftie intellectuals, Common*

Purpose, the BBC, over-zealous Health and Safety officials, "oppressive" shopping malls and, perhaps less expectedly, gymnasiums and health spas. You worry for his blood pressure, for his heart – how long can it take the strain of sustaining this fiery firmament of perpetual rage?'

There were digs at Broadwick's features, his 'extravagant' eyebrows, his posture, his weight (*'his only exercise is the push back – pushing back from the dinner table when he's finished eating'*), his enthusiastic eating style – *'he polishes off his pudding like a starving Somali beggar breaking a week-long fast...he can't sit still, his fingers tap, his knees jiggle...there's the occasional twitch of a muscle in his left cheek when he listens to someone else speaking (with ill-concealed impatience), ever eager to deliver his own unreconstructed Thatcherite certainties.'*

She berated him for not disclosing his salary – *'said to be in the region of £375,000 a year after his esteemed Editor saw off a poaching bid from the Daily Mail'* – and for his feuds with a gay TV comedian, elderly Labour Party statesmen and 'progressive MPs'.

'"Ah diddums," he replies, taunting me aggressively. "Poor little diddums. Did the nasty man tell people the truth about you??? You'll be telling me I should feel sorry for Mr Potato-head" – his nickname for Ian Hislop – "next. Do me a favour Nell. These people dish it out for a living – they just don't like it up 'em!" I bring up the subject of the former Deputy Prime Minister who has stated publicly that he wants to 'smack Broadwick one.' He replies: "If Fat-Boy Prescott still wants to punch me, then that's his problem. Perhaps the great oaf thinks he can mangle me as badly as he does the English language. I'd just like to say through the pages of this august organ that if he ever tries it he'll be going down a lot quicker than Tracey Temple; he'll go down like the Lusitania." Seconds out!'

Broadwick's quotes about his school friends, although accurately reproduced, were accompanied with mocking lines about his social climbing: *'He's stayed in touch with his schoolmates, while leaving them behind financially through his killer combo of ruthless ambition and recycled bigotry. Cue violins! I'm surprised he doesn't break into a rendition of 'My Way'...'*

Butcher's cruellest observation though was aimed firmly below the belt. *'He seems, I think, to blame his wife for their lack of children...even though you feel any competition for her affections would be as welcome in the Broadwick household as a garrulous Jehovah's Witness with African swine fever virus.'*

She acknowledged his audience but claimed they were 'the same people who are drawn to the far-Right' adding that he appeals to *'those who waiver between cynicism and disillusionment, oozing with resentment at the new human values that have left them powerless.'*

Broadwick's attitudes, she concluded, *'have not progressed beyond the 70s – the 1870s. He is a dinosaur, a relic of a nastier age, incapable of natural wit, empathy, originality or imagination. His column is the reason we need press reform. In it, one finds all of the evils of the tabloid press – prurience, prejudice and male insecurity. It is, however, a perfect reflection of William Broadwick. It's judgemental, bigoted, out of place and out of time.'* Ouch.

24

October 15. East Peckham, Kent.

Nobody in the post office noticed the smell, it was Monday morning, benefits day, and the place was awash with peculiar human odours – halitosis, flatulence, unwashed hair and general BO. One small parcel wasn't going to stand out much. It was small, an ornate box beautifully gift-wrapped inside a Jiffy bag which was addressed to Nell Butcher at the *Independent*'s Derry Street office. It was marked personal, and sent by recorded delivery. Inside the box was a present only Gillian McKeith could love – a freshly-laid turd.

25

October 16. Wakefield, Yorkshire. 9am.

Johnny Baker had been awake for two hours, watching season four of *Breaking Bad* on the portable DVD player in his cell. HM Prison Wakefield didn't have much going for it, but at least Category A status meant he had his home comforts, and his little flowery in the Supermax unit was well away from the nonces who had earned the place its Monster Mansion nickname in the red-tops. Real monsters like Sidney Cooke and Levi Bellfield, the creep who murdered Milly Dowler, never crossed John's path. If they did, they'd be brown bread.

Johnny Baker, known as Johnny Too, still had six years to go of his twenty-one year sentence. He had been handed a fifteen year minimum in 2001 for his part in running a South London criminal empire, and as if to rub his nose in it, six years on-top rather than concurrent for the cocaine police found when they had raided his Chislehurst home.

The Baker empire had been built on what Johnny called free enterprise and what the straight world viewed as a massive drugs, prostitution and extortion racket. The end-game had been a bloody shoot-out at a botched warehouse raid the year before. The raid had left his dim, psychotic brother Joey dead, and the surviving members of his mob incarcerated.

According to the press, the Baker gang had either been 'the new Krays' (The *Sun*), 'the new Richardsons' (the more geographically accurate *Daily Mail*), 'the British Sopranos' (the *Daily Star*), 'the last white English crime gang left in London' (the *Daily Express*), or 'Viagra-fuelled Gangsters of Lust' (the *Sunday Sport*), strap-line: 'I Did It Duggie Style' – a reference to the brothers' depraved cousin Douglas 'Dougie The Dog' Richards.

John McVicar explained it better when he told ITN that the Bakers had combined the intelligence and business brain of Charlie Richardson with the unhinged brutality of Ronnie Kray, but respectable opinion was united in the conviction that Johnny Too had to be made an example of.

Life behind bars could be cushty though, if you were one of the acknowledged top dogs of organised crime. Especially when there was the added joy of seeing your old adversaries bumped off. The death of rogue undercover filth Harry 'Tyler'

Dean had been a particularly fond moment. It had kept John buoyant for the best part of five years. Then, just a few months ago, none other than Detective Chief Inspector Gordon Hitchcock, retired, the no-good shit-cunt who had ordered a disastrous raid on his pub, the Ned Kelly, had been nicked as part of Operation Elveden and charged with misconduct in public office for flogging tips to the gutter press. Fuckin' have it!

At 9.05am, Johnny hit pause for his daily prayers. He had a busy morning, the *Guardian* had asked him to write a think-piece about his fellow inmate Michael Peterson, known to the world as Charles Bronson, aka 'Britain's most violent prisoner', whose parole was continually refused. Next year Bronson would have served four decades behind bars, and was most definitely the victim of a corrupt penal system.

His occasional pieces about prison life, the dangers of steroid addiction, injustices such as Hillsborough and the insanity of British drug laws had built him quite a following, ranging from intense young students to women wanting to marry him. Johnny looked at the photo of Maxine Slater, his most regular correspondent, which was his iPad screensaver. She was a peroxide blonde with a dirty mind and a genius level IQ. When he got out of this shithole, she'd be his first port of call – and no doubt, ball.

26

Soho House, Central London. Three hours later.

Jackie had never seen William Broadwick so angry. He'd called her on Sunday from the beer garden of his local pub, twice from his study and five times yesterday, to moan about the Nell Butcher "stitch-up". He was no happier about it now. They sat at a far corner in her local club, as he continued to bang on about the piece. "She couldn't have made me seem more sinister if she'd said I spend my spare time wearing a Fred West mask," he complained.

"You need to stop worrying about it," she soothed. "A prominent right-wing figure is never going to get a good ride from a self-righteous left-wing newspaper, especially from that patronising bitch."

Jackie could never tell him that she had actually found the feature quite funny. The only thing that had wound her up about it was the picture of Willie and Fiona looking like the loving couple they weren't.

"The picture of you as a chubby-faced schoolboy was cute."

He grunted. She went on: "You spoke about damage limitation on the phone, but what possible damage can this cause you? Okay, it confirmed her readers' prejudices about you, but any of your supporters who happened to see it would see Butcher as a sarcastic leftie snob. There was nothing damaging in it for you."

"I tell you what is damaging," he said in a whisper. "These pro-Broadwick protests and meetings. Who are these people?"

"Willie, that's a positive development. The same thing happened with Enoch in the 1970s, ad-hoc groups sprang up, calling themselves Powellites. He didn't encourage them, but he didn't disown them either. It's a good thing, on balance. It shows you've touched a nerve with the man in the street. The party mandarins will love that."

"Well maybe, but when there are demonstrations and violence it could all get out of hand very quickly. I don't want to be publicly identified with street-fighting thugs, so I've made a decision. I'm going to take a break, go over to the Florida Keys with Fiona and let it all die down."

Jackie's face fell like a Basset hound. "When?"

"Immediately. I've spoken to the Editor, it's all cleared."

"A fortnight?" she asked, sulkily.

"Three weeks, maybe a month. That will do the trick. I'll come back to a whole new news agenda. Butcher's poison will be chip paper by then, the protest groups will have polished their jackboots and moved on to some other cause and we can get back to normal."

Jackie pictured the loving couple in bed together, in boats and on the beach. She knew they'd be sharing candle-lit meals and midnight walks, and she also knew then and there that 'normal' would never again be good enough for her – the mistress side of their relationship was more finished than the Liberal Democrats.

"Are you eating?" he asked, more cheerful now.

"Can't," she said, smiling sweetly. "I have to get back to the office, it's hectic this afternoon. I only got out to see you by claiming I had an emergency dental appointment."

She kissed him on the cheek, hiding her disappointment behind a smile.

"Put anything you want on my account and have a good break. I'll see you soon, sexy boy."

Three weeks? Pah. It would only take three minutes for her to put her newly-forming plan into action.

27

Monday, November 12. Wakefield, West Yorkshire

Sausage Fingers Finlay left the frock behind when he visited John Baker in HMP Wakefield. It was probably for the best. His attempts to contact his old cell-mate Dougie the Dog had come to nothing – Richards had apparently come out of nick and with what friends and family had felt to be indecent speed had got straight on a plane to Thailand where he'd shacked up with a child bride within the month; "some bint he'd contacted on the net", according to Slobberin' Ron Sullivan, the former guv'nor of the Bakers' Ned Kelly pub, who volunteered the additional thought "contrary to rumour, it weren't even a lady-boy either, 'cos he's already got a half-chat kid with 'er."

Sausage Fingers had got Slobberin' Ron to set up the prison visit. He had recognised Harry Tyler the minute he'd stepped into the gay club, because Dougie had sellotaped the snidey bastard's newspaper obituary to the wall of their flowery. Finlay knew John Baker needed to be told, and face to face was the only way to do it. The man who'd put Johnny Too in the slammer had balls to even stay in the country.

John had been surprisingly calm about the news and had used the visit to set up a drug deal for a third party. At the end, he'd thanked Sausage Fingers, told him to expect "a nice drink" for his trouble and asked him to report back if he had any further intel about the no-good shit-cunt's whereabouts or associates. There was no rush, though. Time was one thing Baker had in spades. Like a psychotic clown, on the outside he was all smiles, but inside he was seething.

28

William Broadwick was right. A lot can happen in three weeks. The Butcher piece was quickly forgotten, and the UK's news agenda was understandably dominated by the latest wave of Savile revelations.

Gary Shaw kept busy too. His DCI, the SIO (Senior Investigating Officer) of the murder squad, had seen the merit in his unusual idea – and so had the Chief Superintendent, who convinced the Chief Constable, who in turn liaised with the Special Case Work Section of the Crown Prosecution Service. They then approached the Home Office. A plan this bold needed the authority of the Home Secretary, Theresa May, and after much debate and deliberation clearance was given. The word filtered back to Gary Shaw: game on.

29

November 17. Rusholme, Manchester. 4pm

I got to Rusholme early. Kenneth had hired the function room at a hotel near Platt Fields Park for tonight's meeting. For our amusement, he'd booked it under the name of the Anglo-Pakistan Friendship Society. The wag! I'd planned to check the place out in advance but as luck would have it, I never even got to see it.

Parking up, I could hear the sweet innocent laughter of children at play, kids getting the most out of what was left of the sunlight. I glanced over at the small gang of reprobates chasing each other around, they were gurgling away like a country stream in summertime. Suddenly the murmur of contented glee was interrupted by a cry of pain. One little chavvie had come off his BMX bike, and a wild-eyed girl who appeared to be his big sister was giving him a cuddle. I was transfixed. The two kids looked pretty much the same age as my Courtney Rose and Alfie must be now – same height, same hair colouring too. Uncharacteristically, I found my bottom lip trembling and to my absolute horror, I started welling up with tears.

Suppressed thoughts flashed unbidden into my mind, along with long buried regrets. Then the revelation hit me like a wrecking ball: this was the awful price I was paying for staying alive – separation from the ones I loved. An aching sense of sadness overwhelmed me, along with a gnawing loneliness. The pain was almost physical. I did up the car window quickly, put my head on the steering wheel and wept like a *Big Brother* contestant who has just realised that the cameras are on them.

Yeah, this was what I was missing while I was kidding meself that everything was sweet; the precious everyday normality of watching my children grow up. But some other geezer had been driving them to school, taking them to football, doing their homework, tucking them up in bed and kissing their bruises better...

My normal instinct would have been to make a joke of this, maybe say something half witty like nothing is more precious than the laughter of children except the silence of not having any. But not now. Years of sorrow and pent-up emotion flooded out of me in a tsunami of unmanly grief and no doubt self-pity. Harry Tyler – Jack the Lad? No, the big, tough can-do macho man was just another weeping wimp cocooned in a private hell. The Man of Steel had a heart of mush.

It was my fault, of course, for taking the law into my own hands. I had deliberately walked away from civilised society and turned a corner that, short of a miracle, I could never ever walk back around. And although I did not regret ridding the world of those evil slags the Nelsons, I did regret and resent the terrible personal cost.

I squeezed and twisted the knuckles of my left hand hard to pull myself together, dried my eyes and checked my big stupid boat in the rear-view mirror. There was still three hours until the meeting, plenty of time to wash off every embarrassing trace of brine and sink a few jars. In the absence of a punch bag, beer would have to do. It wouldn't take long to get back in the right state of mind...

30

Central London, 4.15pm

Jackie Sutton hailed a taxi outside of the Carlton Club. She looked terrific in a grey mélagne business suit and Vivienne Westwood heels, and she felt immensely pleased with herself. Jackie had spent the past three hours in a blizzard of networking, socialising with Daddy's well-connected friends in the Conservative Party hierarchy, acting as William Broadwick's unofficial agent. She had put on a great show, saying all the right things to all the right people. She'd been waspish, witty and occasionally wise, and as she'd long suspected she was knocking on an open door. The Party readily understood Broadwick's backwoods appeal, his media skills and common sense populist opinions. A Cabinet Minister let her know, off the record, that Cameron's Tories would welcome an official approach from William. It would play well with the Tory Right, who felt utterly betrayed by the wishy-washy compromises Coalition government conveniently necessitated. A safe seat in the Home Counties was William Broadwick's for the asking.

31

Rusholme, Manchester

IT had been more than a month since I'd last seen Katie's father. I'd spent it productively, taking care of business, racking up beer tokens and trying to ration the number of nights she spent round mine. And not only because she'd got hooked on the *Fifty Shades* books and kept on wanting me to act out the scenes either. Listen, I'm not complaining but she had got so demanding I'd had to score black market Viagra just to keep up with her. Funny enough, my local barber supplies 'em at a cockle a pop. It used to be 'Something for the weekend, sir?', now it's something for the weak end...

They were rotten books, as it happened, but to birds they were like every single aphrodisiac known to man concentrated together and converted into words on the printed page. No wonder the Met Office said we'd had the wettest year since records began...

On top of that, alarm bells were ringing. The first major problem was knowing that creepy Ken McManus was not what he seemed, the second was the obvious side-bar that he was going to get noticed by the big boys any day now – things were getting volatile out there in the real world. The ice cream was trouble on a stick, a liability. I couldn't afford to have him anywhere near me – let alone properly wrapped around me...which meant one way or another me and Knockers were going to be strictly a short-term thing. If I ignored those two certainties and just kept him at arms' length then a) she was sharp enough to work out something was wrong, and b) odds-on, when the security services came sniffing around him, everyone around him and his organisation would get looked at in microscopic detail...I could not afford to come under that level of scrutiny. So clearly I had two choices – drop Katie like a red-hot cattle prod or take Ken out of the game myself.

It was some dilemma. If I dropped her, she'd hate me. If I acted on my instincts and helped bring him down, and she found out, she'd probably hate me even more...which was a shame because once or twice, in my weaker moments, I'd found meself thinking we could have been an altar job. We hadn't even had a proper row yet. Bright, sexy, funny, randy...what's not to like? The old man, that's what. It was my own personal Catch 22. Okay, Catch 69 if you must. But if I got him banged up without her knowing, I'd only be postponing the inevitable, playing poker with Fate, buying meself some time.

With all this shit running around my brain, the sensible quick fix solution was alcohol. I'd been told that Hardy's Well was the best battle-cruiser on the Curry Mile, good beer, no ag and friendly staff. The downside was that most of the clientele were scruffy student types, a festering mess of torn jeans, naff T-shirts and naffer jumpers. As I walked in, I spotted old Albert Simmonds sitting at a corner table on his Todd in a dark, chalk-stripe whistle, eating a meat pie and reading the *Daily Mail*. He looked as incongruous as Amy Childs on *Eggheads*.

I made straight for the khazi to wash the pain away and get the Tyler mask back on. Five minutes later, fully composed, I burst back in cheeky Cockney luvaduck 'character' mode. A long-haired layabout was slurping his pint of Guinness carelessly at the bar. Ho! A Yeti! It looked like he and the hedge he'd recently been dragged backwards through had then been dragged under a carpet, in a squat.

A little peroxide blonde sort, quite cute with bad tattoos and a beanie hat, was keeping him from falling off the bar stool.

"Oi, steady on big boy," I said loudly. "Some of that is actually going in your mouth, mate." His girlfriend laughed and I gave her a little wink. Albie heard my voice and beckoned me over. I got myself a lager top on the way, and bought the old fella half a bitter shandy.

"No Katie today?" he asked.

"No, she's on a friend's hen do up town. Dream Boys, daiquiris and dirty dancing apparently."

"Tut. Women today, absolutely shameless."

And thank gawd for that! – was the thought I didn't express. I noticed he had gravy on his chips and felt momentarily queasy.

"Is there a Mrs. Simmonds, Albie?"

"There was, lad, but I lost her."

"I'm sorry to hear that."

"I lost Eunice to heart disease. Iraq took my son, and the banks took my business...It's just me now. I could roll over and play dead, or instead I can do what I'm doing, get involved, prove that there's still some sting in an old bee."

"So politics..."

"Fills the gap, yes. But it's also something I care about, Harry. Modern life is a rigged game, lad; it's rigged against the old, the hard-working, the tax payer, the Christian, the poor bloody infantry. Someone has got to make a stand."

I sipped my beer. "So why not join a party with half a chance of getting elected?" The question hung in the air for a moment. The old man looked at me and scowled.

"What, like Cameron's Tories? They're not Conservative any more, nowhere near it. I was a member once; Enoch was my man, the greatest leader we never had. I completely lost interest in them after that. I would have joined UKIP, but because I stood as a candidate for the National Front back in the Seventies they won't have me..."

"The Front?" I raised an eyebrow. Where was this going?

"I know what you're thinking Harry, but the NF weren't all rotten. There were ex-servicemen and even a rector in our branch. We didn't know that the old leadership had been Hitler-loving creeps. But you live and learn. And because I don't trust the BNP for the same reasons, I'm in Kenny's gang now, for my sins."

"He's got a factory round here hasn't he?" I asked quickly but casually.

"No, no. It's in Wythenshawe, the Roundthorn Industrial Estate."

"And your son, how old was he?"

"27. Kevin was killed during a bomb attack on a military ambulance that was delivering humanitarian aid in Basra...."

"Oh Albie, I'm sorry."

"He's just a statistic now. One of the 179 brave men we lost in the so-called War On Terror that made no sense when it started and even less sense in retrospect. By rights Tony Blair would be on trail as a war criminal at The Hague instead of swanning around the globe coining in millions..."

I nodded enthusiastically and drained my pint. On this at least, he was bang-on. Albert kept going: "But instead we're gearing up for more foreign intervention in the name of God knows what. No Harry lad, I can't get my boy back, but maybe, just maybe, a frail old pensioner can help us get our country back."

He paused, I patted him on the back.

"Let me get another beer in," I said.

"Go on then, I'll have half a Nigerian lager this time, as it's you buying."

Up at the bar, there was an older geezer behind the jump with a face the colour of a smoker's ceiling. Either he was on day release from *The Simpsons* or the bloke had some serious liver disease going on.

I ordered with a smile that was unreturned. He was about as helpful as a Parisian waiter. I looked along the bar. The Yeti didn't look too well. Any greener and he'd start to photosynthesize. The cute little beanie blonde was struggling to keep him from sliding off his stool. I managed to steady him up, then shook him wide awake and wiped the drool from his beard with a Newcastle Brown Ale beer towel.

"I'd take him home if I were you love," I said. "Either that, or dump him in the park for the kids to use as a bouncy castle."

She laughed nervously and thanked me. I paid Homer Simpson and took my pint and Albert's half a Guinness back over to our table, goading him gently to try and open him up.

"I understand what you were saying, Albert, but I still can't see how a few good ol' boys in Manchester hope to make a difference."

"Because it's not just us, Harry," he said, suddenly animated. "There are good old boys like us all over the country, and quite a few young'uns too. Ken is part of a new network. We've just been biding our time to launch nationally, and that will happen within a matter of weeks, now we've got ourselves a figurehead."

"That being...?"

"William Broadwick, the only man in the controlled media with the guts to tell it like it is... 95 per cent of what he says is what we say, and you can bet he's there with us on the other five per cent but wants to keep his job."

"So, is Broadwick in on this?"

"Not yet, but he's in our sights. We've been on to his agent and booked him to speak at a conference in London next month. We spoke his language, hard cash."

"A conference? Very up-market."

"It's called Whither England. It's going to big, lad. There will be hundreds there, from all sorts of different groupings, activists, nationalists, ex-military men, disillusioned councillors from other parties. We've made William's agent an offer that I'd be very surprised if he turned down. But whether he joins us or not, that day will see the birth of a new national organisation, a British people's party..."

Two young men in Stone Island tops came, in eyeing the clientele with ill-disguised contempt. The bigger, angrier Herbert had a face like a clenched fist, but he brightened up when he saw Albert. He got a thumbs up, I got a respectful nod.

"Tonight's security," Albie muttered.

"Do you know Ken well?" I asked casually.

"Not well."

"But you trust him?"

He hesitated. "His heart's in the right place..."

The 'but' hung unsaid in the air.

My mobile buzzed; it was a text from Knockers but it gave me an early exit route. I pulled a face. "Sorry Albie, business," I lied. "I've gotta dash. Apologise to Kenneth for me please."

"No problem, work comes first. Work and family."

That's right, and my work here was done. I shook Albert's hand, drained my pint and left. On the way out I noticed that the Yeti was comatose, and that the security boys had made a move on the blonde. Lucky girl. I needed to process all of this. I couldn't give a flying fuck about the politics, to be honest, and couldn't see it leading anywhere except into more ag. But if what Albie was saying was even half true, it meant I had to leap away from Ken's kin and clan, perhaps spell that with a 'K', as quickly as possible. If they weren't infiltrated now, they soon would be.

I'd like to think that I would spot an MI5 mole before they'd spot me. My colleagues in the U/C game always said I had a magic eye – that I could suss out a wrong'un, a dodge-pot or a fraud within moments of meeting them. I had a knack for it, an instinct that was rarely wrong. But in this situation there was nothing to be gained from calling it on, and everything to be lost.

Outside, I paused and looked at me moby. The text from Knockers was a drunken and misspelt one informing me of her latest carnal desires. I decided not to reply. What I needed to do was go home and start working on an escape route before...

The pub door opened and shut behind me. Their footsteps stopped abruptly. Someone had followed me out. Fist-face?

I turned around warily. Hold up, it was the blonde in the beanie hat...and, as I now saw, an Airbourne T-shirt, boots and black stockings which had been hidden by the Yeti's barrel-sized beer gut. She wasn't half bad in the twilight, if you liked that rock chick sort of thing. And in my experience, not many men don't...

The girl smelt of incense and hash, like Glastonbury on a good day.

"Have you got any vodka back at yours?" she asked. Then she smiled and...you know exactly where this is going, don't you? Trust me. These things happen when you're a good-looking bastard.

32

Monday November 19. Wakefield, West Yorkshire

Gary Shaw was not exactly inspired by Wakefield High-Security Prison. Britain's 'most notorious jail' was largely Victorian, bleak and antiquated, and suffused with a smell that he didn't like but couldn't readily identify. He wasn't too sure that he wanted to, either.

Johnny Baker had been surprised to be summoned to the Governor's office, and was even more shocked to see DI Shaw waiting for him with a cute foxy red-head who he introduced as Detective Sergeant Rhona Watts. Baker had known Shaw from South London and Wattsie would definitely be starring in his next wank. He gave her his most disarming smile.

"Hello my dear. I hope you didn't leave the red light burning in your window, not with the price of electricity these days."

"Cut it out John," Shaw said curtly.

"Or what, Gal? Will you lock me up at Her Majesty's pleasure? Whoops too late, mate, I'm already here."

Baker's presence was sure, his gaze clear; his manner cruised straight through easy confidence to ring the bell marked bullish bonhomie. Sensing the DI's unease, Johnny chased his advantage with a cheap shot one-liner. "Besides, you're the ones who claim to have a 'Special Escort' Group..."

He hadn't got any less gobby then, Shaw thought. He gave the grinning gangster a look he could have whittled wood with, but Wattsie laughed it off. "It's okay, guv, my red light runs on a meter these days," she joked. "On account of the recession."

Baker chuckled and winked. "What are the odds of a double dip then, luv? Maybe get the old prison governess involved, see how filthy The Filth can get..."

"Oh we can offer you something a bit better than that, Mr Baker," she said, coquettishly. "How would you like to go all the way? All the way out of here?"

For once Johnny Too bit his lip and listened as the two cops brought him up to speed on the killings, and the suspected link to William Broadwick's column. They had yet to find any worthwhile forensic evidence, except for unidentified female hair in the back of one murder victim's car in Essex; however eye witness accounts all put the suspect as an athletic male about 5ft 8, 5ft 9.

"So he could have an accomplice..."

"Or the barnet could be a red herring," said Johnny Too who had already sussed out where this was going. "And you want a bigger fish to dangle to tempt the perpetrator out into the open in a controlled situation."

"Bang on," said Gary Shaw. "The biggest fish – Britain's Number One celebrity gangster. You! Broadwick's editor will gee him up to go ballistic about the failings of our extravagantly lenient justice system, the live bait will be cast..."

Johnny finished his sentence."And your fish will be reeled in and landed by Sir Robert Peel's finest sons. Job done."

Baker sat back in his chair and smiled ever wider. "So what's in it for me?" he asked simply.

"Liberty, John. Pretty much immediate release," Shaw explained. "Once you've done your bit and we've got our man, you'll be back on Civvy Street. Free as a bird."

"How will that work?"

"We're working through the cover story with the Home Office," said Rhona Watts. "It'll be water-tight though – miscarriage of justice involving the extra sentence you got following the raid on your home, which, coupled with your impeccable behaviour inside, will mean that with her Solomon-like wisdom, Home Secretary Theresa May will see fit to order your immediate release."

"Under our control, until the job is done," Gary Shaw added quickly.

"It's a good offer," said Johnny, his blue eyes twinkling. "And I'm up for it. There's just one condition..."

33

Wednesday, November 21. Woking, Surrey, 10am.

William Broadwick hung up quickly and turned off his mobile phone. He'd only been back in the country for twenty-two hours and Jackie had already rung him thirteen times. Of course he'd ring her back and see her soon, but there were things that had to be done – he'd come back to a mountain of messages, and a treasure trove of emails offering paid work. He had to sort his diary out – his speaking engagements had gone through the roof! Besides, hadn't she heard of jet-lag for God's sake?

Benjamin Franklin had got it wrong, he decided. There were three certainties in a man's life – death, taxation and women giving you grief.

Fiona found him on the living room settee twenty minutes later, lounging about in his ancient paisley y-fronts, the most unflattering pants known to man, reading the morning's papers. She laid his breakfast tray next to him. He wasn't a pretty sight, thought Fiona, what with the man-boobs and paunch, but at least he was hers.

Broadwick grunted "thanks" and reached for his favourite bacon and egg sandwich, heavy with Daddy's Sauce.

"I don't like the *Sun* on a Wednesday," he said, with melted butter running down his cheeks. "In fact I don't like any of their columnists much any more. Ally Ross is good, on the odd weeks he bothers to write, but Clarkson's weekend column is first-thought stuff, Frankie Boyle is a disgrace, Jane Moore is no Jan Moir, and Rod Liddle never quite gets the tone right. He looks nothing like his by-line picture either, in real life he looks more like a large toad-faced sloth."

"Oh I like Jane Moore," protested Fiona.

"It's a lazy column. Very little effort. Other people's jokes. The serious stuff is never more than okay. She probably knocks it out in an hour and a half. It never makes you sit up and think 'wow, that took guts to write' – and you did think that with Jean Rook and occasionally Lynda Lee-Potter, and still do with Melanie Phillips."

"Lorraine Kelly?"

"Pathetic. The only one who's always spot-on is Trevor Kavanagh. You get the feeling that he is Murdoch's emissary on earth."

"Willie..."

She was changing the subject. Her tone made him wary. "Yes?"

"Are we still okay for Saturday the 8th?"

"Saturday the 8th?" He feigned ignorance.

"The reunion!"

"Oh, yes, well, if you insist."

She reached over and pecked him on the forehead. "Good boy," she said softly before she stood back, opened her dressing gown and revealed stockings, suspenders and a black lace-up corset. "And good boys deserve treats."

Broadwick groaned inwardly but forced a smile. "Lovely," he said. "Give me half an hour for my breakfast to go down."

She smiled and retreated upstairs. He darted to his office and took half of a Viagra tablet. It was important to go through the motions, keep his wife happy, but she never turned him on the way Jackie did. He looked around his office walls, covered with his own laminated columns and framed cartoons depicting him. Some of them, the ones from the *Guardian* and *Independent* were quite cruel. But they reminded him of how far he had got, how much he had achieved. So yes, he'd pop pills to keep the little woman happy as long as he could have Jackie as a just reward for his rising profile. He'd have to have a serious talk with her soon, though. She was getting too demanding, too clingy. She had to know that the way they were would be the only way they could ever be.

34

London, Soho House. Seven hours later

Joanna Sutton kissed her cousin on both cheeks and launched into a tirade of greetings, half-thoughts and asides delivered so quickly they could easily have been mistaken for gobbledegook or Klingon.

The music biz PR was one of nature's heat-seeking missiles: hard to avoid, occasionally mesmerising and always explosive. She was magnificently cool, with the curves of Christina Hendricks. Her blonde mane was expertly bouffed, her fingers sparkled with diamonds, her cleavage was dusted with glittery powder. Even in the jaded heart of Soho, Jo Sutton turned heads.

"Lovely to see you, Jackie. Mwah, mwah. God, you're still gorgeous. Hmm. Cocktails! Yes. Let's order. I've had a frightful day, I've had a mare with Celine's people in Hollywood, still got problems with the accountant over the tax return – have you got any spare receipts by the way? Frightful minicab ride here too. Little Paki driver was like halitosis in a suit. REEKED! Kept trying to talk to me, jabber-jabber-jabber vawt-vawt-vawt....Speak ENGLISH you MORON! Got lost twice, probably hasn't passed his test, and then expected me to give him a tip. I told him SUCK MY FUCKIN' DICK, creepoid. Anyway, how are you baby cakes?"

Jackie started to speak, then felt her face start to crumple. Jo was over in a second, slinging a protective arm around her. Jackie started to sob.

"Not here," whispered Jo. She ushered her into the ladies where the tears really came into their own.

"Is it Willie?"

"Oh Jo, I, I..."

"Sssh, babes, come on, take your time."

"He makes me so mad, I do everything for him. I've pulled so many strings for him. I love him like crazy, and he treats me like crap."

"What's he done now?"

"He won't return my calls, Jo, he won't even take them."

"Arrogant shit."

"I wouldn't mind, except he tells me he loves me. I've got family friends, people you know well, who want to sit down with him and make all of his dreams come true...and, and..."

"So you're still together?"

"Sort of. I think. We were going at it hammer and tongs until he went off on holiday."

"With that cow Fiona?"

"Yes."

"With the problem calves?"

"Yes." A smile.

"So he's had a nice vacation with Her Indoors, realised he doesn't really want to rock the boat at home, and..."

"He's trying to cool us down, I think."

"If I know William, and I think I do, I've certainly known a lot of men like him, then I expect what he really wants is to stay married and keep you as his bit on the side."

"I don't want that, though Jo. It's not good enough."

Joanna's demeanour changed. Her eyes turned cold, her face was now stiffened with steely resolve as well as Botox.

"No, it isn't," she said slowly. "Who wants to be old saggy bollocks' mistress? You deserve much more, my girl. Give me five minutes, there's someone I want you to meet."

In the event, Holly Kirpachi turned up forty minutes later. Jo introduced her as "Fleet Street's hottest showbiz reporter," adding mischievously "I thought you two should get together. Jackie knows everyone worth knowing in Parliament, Holly, and you can't write about Olly Murs all your life...and Jackie maybe you'll need a friend with the power to break stories one day, you never know."

Holly shook Jackie's hand. "Call me Bang Bang," she said. She was a striking Anglo-Asian girl with an Essex accent, long dark hair and teeth that would dazzle an Osmond. Jo ordered "a gallon of lady petrol" – three bottles of Ruinart Blanc de Blancs, Brut NV. Jackie cheered up remarkably quickly.

35

Johnny Too had only demanded two things; the easy bit was he wanted to liaise with Gary Shaw, and only Shaw, throughout the sting operation. The hard part was he wanted Harry Tyler to be his close protection officer.

"But Tyler's dead," the baffled DI had replied. Johnny Baker told him all about Sausage Fingers Finlay's encounter with the ghost of the Met's best in Blackpool. Shaw, still baffled, had said he'd look into it.

On the train back to London Kings Cross, he googled Harry Tyler's obituaries on Wattsie's iPad. All of the nationals had faithfully reproduced the official MI5 sanctioned line that Tyler, real name Harry Aaron Dean, had been an undercover officer who had died in the course of an on-going investigation. All of them mentioned that he had been recommended posthumously for the Queen's Police Medal for gallantry, but the details of his death – the crucial where, when, why and how – had not been disclosed. It all had the whiff of cover-up, thought Shaw.

Rhona Watts looked at the headshot of Tyler in uniform. "He's fit," was her verdict. "But why is he dead, if he isn't?"

"I'm really not sure."

"Could he have gone rogue?"

"A few of them do. I heard of one U/C guy, Mark Moody, about ten years back who started doing private work importing large quantities of class A narcotics for organised crime gangs. He got away with it for nearly a year and a half, because he could travel in and out of the country with impunity, using the shield of genuine police operations. He ended up being monitored 24/7 by the Spooks, but got out of it before anyone could bring him down. Lives in Mazzaron apparently. Another one who was suspected of transporting Charlie, Kev Hanscombe, works as an emergency defence lawyer in Loughton now. The firm, get this, is called Sidney Springer & Partners – Sid, CID, and Springer because they're all ex Old Bill and they're all earning twice as much now working for the dark side springing villains, shoplifters and piss-taking travellers as they ever did batting for our team."

Wattsie grimaced. "Okay, so if Tyler had gone rotten, and hadn't wrangled his pension before he got found out...or if he's on Witness Protection...or off working for OGA...or been seconded for a long-term deep cover op..."

"Who knows, Rhon? There are umpteen possible explanations for what's gone on and why he's still alive when the world thinks he's croaked. All I know for certain is we'll have to kick this upstairs. If Harry's alive, someone at MI5 or GCHQ will know. And if we need him on side, then we'll need top level clearance to get him there. Strings will have to be pulled – and quickly."

36

Friday, November 23.Manchester, 6pm.

I'd bowled in to Jolly Butcher half an hour ago, just having a nose to be honest. It was the nearest boozer to the Roundthorn Industry Estate, a functional but ugly outcrop of twenty-odd business units.

The barmaid's face told a thousand stories, none of them good, so I'd struck up a conversation with a couple of guys from a struggling stationery supply firm. Turned out that they were based pretty much next door to dear old Kenneth's warehouse, and surprise surprise, they reckoned the workers there were mostly Romanian and probably illegal. I'd definitely have a sniff about. A would-be politician, wrapped in the English flag, using illegal immigrant labour? If the word got out, it would nobble his plans as effectively as slipping a groom a bromide daiquiri on his wedding night. More importantly, the UK Border Agency would get Ken at least a two stretch quicker than you could say porridge.

37

Pembury, Kent. Four hours later.

The hotel was two stars. It was the first thing that Jackie had noticed. It was their first night together since their break, and Willie had taken her to a drab little hole outside Tonbridge that cost him £69 a night. It was the only 69 that would come up tonight as well, she was sure about that. It wasn't like he was even paying for it, the paper was. Broadwick had come to Kent to do "vital research for the column" – a good excuse for a night away from the missus, granted, but why not treat her to a night in Danehurst House? The answer was so blindingly obvious, she didn't even have to ask – there was less chance of anyone who "mattered" seeing them here, or in the insultingly bog standard burgers and ribs pub restaurant he'd taken her to beforehand. That was what she was to him now, a cheap leg-over; something he could take for granted. He booked a functional hotel for his functional whore. Well, things wouldn't stay that way for too much longer.

Jackie played her pompous lover like a master puppeteer, teasing him all night with promises, touching him under the table, making sure he drank so much that he became indiscreet, and then so much more that he'd be incapable of the sex she no longer felt like allowing him. In the morning he came to with a hangover that was as hard to avoid as his increasingly hoary hard-on. Broadwick had little recollection of any of the previous night's conversations. He did not remember Jackie talking about all of his former school-friends in great detail, or letting on which ones he didn't like and more crucially telling her which disgruntled old chum would most like to see the great man's world of lucrative infamy collapse on him.

He certainly didn't see the female photographer with the Nikon D3200 night lens camera take some surprisingly good shots of them snogging in the car park, entering the hotel arm in arm and leaving together all smiles the next morning. Bang-bang! Bang-bang! Bang-bang!

38

I'd popped into the Oak for a pie and a pint. The plan was to read the paper, pick out a few horses and have a leisurely afternoon indoors with me feet up watching Channel 4 Racing. In the event, the small message in the *Telegraph*'s Announcements section changed all of that.

The message consisted of just six simple coded words, but it was enough to stop me dead in my tracks. I re-read them seven or eight times, letting their meaning sink in. Then I clicked into action. Suddenly, my heart was racing. I left the pint, picked up a cheap Nokia 2600 pre-paid mobile and drove over to Woodheys Park to make a call I'd dreamt about making for more than ten years.

The conversation was short, clipped, largely oblique and almost too good to be true. The second part of it would be conducted face to face in a location of my choosing and entirely on my terms. There were dogs with two dicks who didn't feel as chuffed as I currently did. So what was the catch? I couldn't afford to be too trusting, not yet. These people played by their own rules.

I dumped the phone in a dog-shit bin and drove randomly for miles, thinking things over with just a Sam Cooke's CD for company. A Change Is Gonna Come indeed.

I ended up in Penketh, Warrington, in a cosy good-value Italian called Delgados. By the time the 10oz pepper steak arrived, medium rare as requested, I'd made up my mind. The second bottle of Barolo was just for celebration. The third, on the house from restaurateur Julie, put the tin hat on it. I may have slept in the car, but I slept happy.

39

Sunday 25 November, 2pm. The French House, Soho

Holly Kirpachi was already drinking Breton cider at the bar when Jackie Sutton arrived. Jackie ordered a 2007 bottle of Pouilly-Fuissé Monternot and ushered Bang Bang away from a small group of slightly whiffy admirers. In the corner of the small pub, they talked intently but in near whispers. Jackie gave the reporter a name and a phone number. "He's the one," she said simply.

40

Wednesday 28 November, Tonbridge, Kent, 1.55pm

Gary Shaw had disappeared up to London for various secret squirrel meetings; he was due back for an up-date sometime this afternoon. Detective Sergeant Wattsie Watts had put the DI's crossword to one side a while ago and had started scribbling on her notepad. She wrote out letters, then crossed them out and wrote out the same letters in a different order again and again, until she found what she had been looking for.

Shaw had come back unannounced and thought he'd caught Rhona doodling. He was just about to bollock her when she showed him the list of crossings out that led from 'Cam O'Dolland' to 'Old MacDonald'. She then did the same trick with 'Miles Farger' and found 'Farmer Giles' even faster.

"It could be a red herring, guv," she said. "Or..."

"Or it could be that the man we want, the mystery man in the flat cap, is telling us he's a farmer," he said. "Which narrows the suspects down to what? About 330,000?"

"Probably a few hundred in easy striking distance of here," noted Rhona.

"Too many," said Gary Shaw. "Farmer fucking Giles. He's rubbing our noses in it."

41

Friday 30 November, London. The West End.

I was due to meet Johnny Too in Quo Vadis in Soho, but en route I got a text saying to meet in the snug bar of the Angel, a Sam Smiths pub in St Giles High Street first. It was a standard trick, change the location at the drop of the hat to give the other side less chance to secrete hidden cameras around the gaff. I'd done it twice when I'd met Gary Shaw with the SO13 boys on Wednesday. I'd gone with my brief, plus I'd had an old mate on standby around the corner. Leroy McLellan, one of the hardest-punching heavyweights ever to come out of the Lynn AC gym,; forty-four professionals wins, thirty-eight by knock-outs. As it happened, it would have made more sense for me to have brought him with me tonight...

Johnny was in the pub ahead of me. Up at the bar, knocking back organic cider, his shoulders wide enough for two prop forwards. When he saw me, John flashed a smile that didn't quite reach those mesmerising blues eyes.

I held my hand out to shake his, but it had already curled into a big wrecking ball of a fist that was coming straight at me. Fuck. I ducked back quickly enough to miss the full impact, but not fast enough to swerve it entirely. I caught the wall to stop myself falling and launched back at him with all I had.

The next four minutes were the hardest of my life. Baker was always strong, but now he was strong and fit – all those hours in the prison gym had worked wonders.

I was glad the old footwork hadn't entirely deserted me, and that he'd clearly had a few.

Panting, Johnny had my throat between his thumb and forefinger, pinching, pressing choking...the room started to swim. But then my anger energized me. I grabbed his right hand with my left and started to crush it. Now his face curdled in pain. I wrenched his hand away, squeezing it with reserves of strength I didn't know I had. I chinned him hard with my right, kneeing him in the bollocks as he staggered back. Gasping, he clawed at my face, like a girl, and grabbed me in a bear hug. John tripped me up backwards and slammed my face down on the Axminster. Not the sort of rug-munching I had in mind on a night out.

It took two barmen and a couple of Spurs geezers from the saloon bar to pull us apart. I can't say I wasn't grateful. If I'd ever been in a harder fight, the memory of it had been knocked clean out of my brain. It was like going two rounds with Adrien Broner. And now look at me – I was panting like some old sixty-a-day crone with emphysema, trying to spit the taste of pub carpet out of my mouth.

"That was for Joey, you understand?" Johnny spat. He glared at the men holding him, who released their grip immediately.

I waited for the "and for Dougie and for Geraldine" – but the words didn't come. Did he even know about Geri? Something else to worry about... Nothing was broken, but I had a cracked tooth and my neck felt numb. Both of our faces were bruised and swollen from blows. I was no slouch when it came to a ruck, but I'd felt a bit like The Thing when he had to take on The Hulk (*'Page after page of pulse-pounding thrills!'* as I recall) – fighting gamely in completely the wrong weight division. Not that I would ever have backed down to the dirty Millwall cowson.

"Are we going to be okay, John?" I asked.

"Good as gold, mate. Just wanted to clear the air, know what I mean? Besides, I have to get on with you and do this thing...it's the condition of me getting out. Afterwards, who knows?" He turned on the bar staff. "What are you fuckin' looking at? Divs! Ain't you seen geezers have a tear-up before? For fucks sake! People getting upset about a little bit of fighting! How do they think we got an empire? At least he reacted like a man and fought back. Come on H. Let's get a proper beer."

Johnny Too's whole demeanour had changed. To carry on The Hulk analogy, it was as if the big green guy had instantaneously morphed back into nice bright affable Bruce Banner.

Fuck me, next time I come out with this lunatic, remind me to pack a cosh.

John walked out of the pub like nothing had happened and turned left, walking towards Soho via Denmark Street. I shrugged, wiped my mouth and caught up with him.

A mob of punky birds, all ripped fishnets and bad hair, had come filing out of the Intrepid Fox and started crossing St Giles High Street. They were in their late twenties and early

Garry Bushell

thirties. Once you looked past the weird corpse make-up and the fact that one of them appeared to be wearing half a pawn shop, they weren't bad looking. The women were covered in slogans: 'She's taken, we're not', 'Future trophy bride', 'Final fling before the ring', 'Buy me a shot, I'm tying the knot' and so on.

"A hen night," I said, dumbly.

"Nice one, Columbo. I can see how you got the job."

"I'm trained to observe...miss."

Baker smiled. "Here H, I know we were going to eat but I'm thinking let's hold the steak and go for pussy."

"I'm with you, bro, either way I'm gonna love chewing the gristle."

A beautiful line, I felt, redolent of Casanova at his most romantic... The women were heading for the 12 Bar club.

"Barnet Mark still run this gaff?" John asked me.

"I couldn't tell you, John. Don't think I've been here since the Libertines played it."

He walked to the front of the queue. "You got any Chelsea slags in here?" he said menacingly to the greasy-haired rockabilly in the Cock Sparrer T-shirt taking money at the door.

"Johnny Too! Fuck me!"

"Barnet, you old tart! Who's on tonight? No West Ham shit, I trust."

"No, it's a Ska night. Jennie Bellestar, 1-Stop-Experience. Fuck me, John. It's been years..."

"Thanks for reminding me."

"Sorry, mate. Do you know John King?"

Barnet clasped his arm around a smart, self-assured man in a combat jacket with a Chelsea badge on his lapel.

"The writer? No! Nice to meet you John, I read all your books inside. Loved *England Away*. This is Harry, Harry Tyler. He's had a good hiding with the ugly stick, the poor bastard, but we go back a way."

Cock Sparrer's song 'Secret Army' was playing over the sound system, which seemed pretty apt. I had a chat with the author, both of us admiring the club's framed selection of old music press covers, while Johnny turned his charm on the hen party, treating them to buckets of innuendo and champagne on ice. The man was as smooth as plate glass, albeit much harder to punch a hole through.

By the time we'd reached the stage area, we'd amassed a crowd of hangers-on, including a dealer, Jennie 'Bellestar' Matthias from the One-Stop-Experience, most of the hens and sultry Carly, the raven-haired bride-to-be, with her head-turning bee-hive and dangling gold hoops that would have given Fat Pat Butcher cause for concern. "One hen and twelve chicks in search of some old cock," John had said, with such a disarming smile that none of them had minded. Barnet closed off the top balcony for our party...

42

Saturday 22nd[h] November. Eltham, South East London. 9am.

Holly Kirpachi knocked at the council house door. The unshaven, middle-aged occupant was in his dressing gown and initially reluctant to let her in. It was too early, he moaned. A flash of her smile, followed by a flash of her cheque book, was all it took. Bang, bang!

43

Central London

We woke up, or perhaps I should say came to, at 9.30am the next morning in a suite at the Covent Garden Hotel in Monmouth Street. Johnny was in bed with bride-to-be Carly and her spaniel-eyed limpet friend. I appeared to have ended up with Rosie, a rockabilly barmaid. My mouth was as dry as a tramp's flannel, my neck was still sore and the tooth hurt like buggery. Only the aching head and the back full of scratches hinted at the night of drunken exertion and coke-fuelled contortion that had been wiped from my memory. Even half-asleep, Carly looked gorgeous. Like a young Salma Hayek, I'd thought last night, but most of her colouring was now decorating Johnny's pillow, and the classy coiffed bee-hive hair was currently more Giant Haystacks than sultry Hayek.

"Have you girls got to be anywhere?" I asked, adding innocently "Like a church?"

The bride-to-be blushed for good reason. "Oh Christ," she shrieked. "Oh shit! Oh shitting, fucking hell!"

"Easy," said Johnny, with a smile. "Put the cuckoo back in the clock, love. Where have you got to be?"

"Bromley."

"Kent or By Bow?"

"Kent. It's more Bickley, St George's Church."

"By?"

"Wedding's at 2 o'clock."

"So panic over, you've got hours. Get yer stuff, I'll call you a sherbert. You'll be home, or wherever you want to be, in half an hour. Plenty of time for a fresh coat of spray-paint or whatever else you need to do. You'll look lovely. You do already."

Johnny spoke with such easy authority that he seemed to suck the alarm straight out of her.

Carly and the near-mute Tracey were gone in under fifteen minutes, and remarkably Rosie slept right through it.

She was a good-looking sort; nicely curvy with an old-fashioned swallow tattooed above her left breast. Now I thought about it, an old-fashioned swallow had featured in our fun and games last night, too.

Slowly the memories returned – Rosie behind the jump, in the fifties style polka dot red and black swing prom pin-up dress that currently decorated the TV set. She caught my eye as effortlessly as Collingwood dismissing Matthew Hayden in 2005. Rosie was generously busty, a pretty brunette in her mid-20s with heavy shaped eyebrows and heavier roulette red lipstick. She looked like someone out of a time machine: old-fashioned, pure and untouched...which had made fucking her so much more fun.

Johnny yawned theatrically as he closed the door on his conquests, looked at me and said "Breakfast?"

"Don't mind if I do. Rosie? Rose?" I nudged her gently.

The barmaid's eyelids flicked. Her double wing eye make-up was heavily smudged; the lipstick had been completely worn off. She smiled and stroked my cheek. I kissed hers.

"You two!" she grinned in a voice from the North West – not quite Manchester or Chester, maybe Runcorn. I'd have to ask. "You were steaming! If I'd written down your conversation last night it would have looked like someone had cut up a Tarantino script and turned it into a ransom note..."

"Ha! When was this?" asked Johnny.

"It was after we'd all been to bed once, and then you and Harry got up and started drinking the Buckfast."

"Buckfast?!" we said as one.

"That Tracey girl had it in her bag."

Rosie modestly pulled the duvet around her ample form and retreated to the khazi. I covered my modesty with a pillow.

"How was it?" Johnny asked reasonably quietly.

I gave him the thumbs up. "Yorn?"

"My first vajazzle," he laughed. "At first I thought it was her price list in Braille."

"Ha. In my day a cunt covered in jewellery was called Jimmy Savile."

"Boom boom!" John smiled contentedly, he looked as happy as a louse in a hobo's chest hair. "She took my number. She reckoned she'd never come like she did last night, or as often. I think I might have taken the shine off the honeymoon, bruv. Not to mention the marriage."

"You mean..."

"She was happy to assume I'd had the snip. But my troops have never been sent on a suicide mission, know what I mean? The world needs more Johnny Toos... Her mate was on the pill, but she weren't much cop. Normally if you wanted sex that dull you'd have to get married."

I smiled. "They do reckon that the most frequent position for married couples is doggie style – the husband sits up and begs, the missus rolls over and plays dead...one of the reasons I won't be walking up any aisles again in a hurry."

My iPhone bleeped. Knockers. I'd had four texts and three missed calls from her since last night. No drama, she knew I was "away on business". She'd wait.

"My old woman divorced me while I was inside," Johnny said, matter of factly, with barely a trace of sadness. "Sold the Chislehurst gaff, changed her name and fucked off to Portugal with some time sleazy share salesman. Dale Bishop. So him and me will be having a nice friendly chat when this is all done and dusted. Though to be honest he's done me a favour. I'm well shot of the old joy vacuum." He paused for a beat. "They've got a villa in Martinhal, near Sagres. Easy enough for me to find out exactly where, 'cos Slobberin' Ron does her mum's plumbing." He paused and looked almost sympathetic. "I heard all about your ex-wives, H – the Filth filled me in. Sorry about Dawn. And was it Kara?"

"Yeah, she still thinks I'm brown bread. I've no idea where she and the kids are, or who she's with. Probably some 9-5 office sap. She always wanted to be 'normal'. I guess I'll find out when this is over, too."

I wondered for a moment what had become of his old barmaid, Lesley Gore. The moment passed.

"But first we're going to flush out the vigilante..." he said.

"Yep. You're the prize John, and I'm your minder. Like you fuckin' need one. But we'll flush him out all right. The story of your release is gonna be front page news in all the Sunday papers this weekend, and this prick Broadwick will be primed by his editor to lead his Tuesday column on the big scandal, setting you up nicely as the trophy at your high-profile release party next Friday."

"At Stringfellow's?"

"If that's where you want it. The location will be revealed on Monday in a tabloid exclusive, the controversy will start to rage, with your chums at the *Guardian* trumpeting your early release as a triumph for British justice. And all week there will be a drip-drip of names of celebrities coming to your liberation knees-up. Our vigilante nutter will be incandescent with rage.

There's no way on earth he'll be able to resist. But of course half the people at the do will be undercover Old Bill, just waiting for him to make his move." I slipped into my best Mr T voice to add: "I pity the foo'."

"Ha," John said, mimicking the accent. "I love it when a plan comes together..."

"Well I've got one of me own, mate. 'Scuse me, John, I will have breakfast, but first I'm going have what you can't. A little morning glory..."

And I sauntered off to the shower with the pillow still covering the evidence, cheerfully singing "Everything's coming up Rosie's..."

***

We emerged 40, 45 minutes later after I'd shown her a new use for a shower attachment. Johnny Too was dressed and beaming. "Breakfast is served," he announced grandly, indicating three bottles of full-fat Coca Cola, a percolator full of hot coffee, three lines of Charlie and three glasses of bourbon.

I passed on everything except the Black Doctor, Coca Cola is always the best hangover cure and I had a lot on today. I had to get to Scotland Yard for a briefing. I had to meet a trustworthy brief. I had to call Knockers. But first and foremost I had to find an emergency dentist.

44

Monday 3rd December. Lower Thames Street, London EC3

The *Daily Express* Editor Paul Lloyd got straight onto William Broadwick as soon as he got into the office. He'd been expecting the big story to break of course, and he played his part in the plan exactly as the Chief Inspector had suggested. The premature release of South London crime lord John Baker was a scandal by any reckoning, but by the time he'd finished ranting about it to his now equally irate star writer there was no doubt about how tomorrow's column would read.

"Batton down the hatches," he laughed to his PA. "Ten tons of horse shit is about to hit the wind turbine."

45

Gary Shaw settled down at his desk with a copy of the *Daily Express*, as usual. Only one thing was different. Today he was actually looking forward to the William Broadwick column, and he didn't disappoint. Willie had led a spectacularly ill-tempered page with a savage assault on Johnny Too's release, with additional thoughts on the uselessness of modern courts and the glorification of criminal scum by contemporary lads' culture. His targets included Great Train Robbers – "dribbling failures", David Courtney – "the wannabe villain with a head like a circumcised manhood", Frankie Fraser – "a psychopathic rat-bag with no conscience and no remorse", and the publisher John Blake, whom he blamed for launching the "ghoulish" criminal autobiography "racket" with his big-selling ghost written books on Lenny McLean and Roy Shaw. The bulk of his vitriol was of course reserved for John Baker (he refused to use his 'Johnny Too' nickname) who was described as "a swaggering, cocksure slime-ball" and "the ugly face of Sarf Lunden black market capitalism repulsively elevated to the status of guru by the wet, liberal voyeurs of the Guardian and trendy Channel 4 wannabes."Shaw smiled. It had gone exactly as planned.

The second lead was devoted to attacking Elf & Safety zealots (a joke he never tired of) for cancelling a Battle Of Turnham Green reunion event. There was a short piece lambasting the public for "pig-ignorant" punctuation howlers – he singled out a greengrocer's sign advertising 'asparagu's' and a hitchhiker who had spelt Hastings 'Hasting's'. Across the bottom of the column was a 150-word rant calling on David Cameron to "put a bomb under the EU" by vetoing the forthcoming European Union budget. Nothing to worry about there, thought Shaw. All he had to do now was lay in wait for Land Rover Man to attempt to gatecrash Johnny Too's release party on Friday night.

46

Thursday 6th December

Toad Rock had attracted some strange people since the murder: ghouls, morbid sightseers, and tonight, a pro-Broadwick gathering. Gary Shaw had started dropping in to the Retreat for inspiration and cask beer. He wasn't happy to find the pub busy and the solitary barmaid didn't look too chuffed either.

Thelma had been watching an argument between two men get out of hand. One, with wingnut ears, had voiced his objection to what he called "the cult of vigilante thickoes". A pro-Broadwick campaigner with glasses and a round face had questioned his parenthood and they were now circling each other, arms wide, in a traditional pre-fight ritual. It started quickly and ended quicker, with Wingnut pulling a ju-jitsu move on his opponent and putting him on his back. Gary Shaw stepped in to finish it there, only for another beefy pro-Broadwick brawler to come flying at Wingnut and crown him with a heavy wooden chair. He went down like a poleaxed ox.

"Enough!" snapped Shaw. For a moment the authority in his voice brought the aggro to a halt, but only for a moment. Suddenly, the guy with the round face was back on his feet and tearing into the DI with a flurry of kidney punches. Mick Neale walked in to see Gary Shaw hit the deck. Thelma screamed, Mick got angry.

"Time to go, ladies," he said firmly.

"Who died and made you Sheriff, Mick?" Beefy asked sarcastically.

Mick could have talked to him, reasoned with him, calmed him down. But the truth was he'd had a long hard day and seeing the tears in Thelma's eyes had done little to alleviate his mood. He drew a police-issue expandable baton from the inside of his coat and whacked the guy straight round the canister. Bosh. Beefy went down like the Belgrano.

"Anyone else want any?" Mick said loudly. "You?" he asked the kidney puncher. "No? Well I suggest you fuck off now and let decent people drink in peace."

Nobody argued. It was worth it, thought Mick, for Thelma's grateful kiss and cuddle, not to mention the free pints.

The off-duty cop was picking himself off the floor.

"You okay?" Mick asked.

"I'll live." He held out a hand. "Detective Inspector Gary Shaw. We have met, Michael, a long time ago. I won't ask about the baton..."

They sat at a corner table and demolished a bottle of Glenfiddich Special Reserve, the ex-cop and the serving DI just shooting the breeze. Shaw brought up 'Farmer Giles'.

"I know you work on a few farms now, Mick," he said. "Can you think of anyone around her dumb or crazy enough to be pulling these stunts?"

Mick took a sip of single malt and savoured the sniff of pear, and the mix of pine, peat and rich fruit on his tongue.

"If you asked me that last month, I'd have said yes, Gary. I would have taken you straight round to Gulliver Stevens. But I saw him the other day and he's lost it. The old man has got bats in his head. We're talking proper loony tunes. No, there's no one like that around here. Maybe old man Ashbee. But no one else."

"Tell me about Ashbee."

"Medium height, hard as a tray of nails, stocky, late fifties, maybe early sixties. Outspoken, a loner, doesn't suffer fools. I don't think this is his style though."

"Does he drive a Land Rover?"

"Most of them do."

At 11.15pm Thelma shut up shop and asked Mick to walk her home as she was shaken up by the fight. He shook hands with Gary Shaw and did his chivalrous duty. On the way she pulled herself into him, enjoying the wiry hardness of his body. They went inside for "a nightcap" and she found him on the settee five minutes later, dead to the world. He was still there snoring at half past nine the next morning.

47

Friday 7th December.Central London. 1am

The explosion that rocked Europe House in London's Smith Square was a home-made device, a fertiliser bomb activated by a crude timer. It had been designed to simply blow out the windows. Unfortunately, a young clubber called Dom Wilson had been walking past at the time. He caught the full blast.

48

Peckham, South London, one hour later.

Bisho's was the sort of club where they have to know you on the door before you come in, one where if you play up you're likely to leave through the back door in a bin-liner. The run-down streets outside were in stark contrast to the Mark Powell suits and discreet but pricey Tom on show in side. If the double-breasted whistle said '67, the face said 10-12. Naturally, Johnny knew everybody, every broken nose and ugly Mars bar in the joint. I recognised a few faces, but mercifully there didn't appear to be anyone here who I'd turned over.

The place was crawling with crooks, conmen, fences, gamblers and their groupies. How many hours of my life had I whiled away in the company of preening, wannabe goodfellas like these, every one of them as delusional as they were undesirable, all in the noble pursuit of law and order? The brotherhood of crime? Bollocks. They were all in it for themselves. A brotherhood of rats.

Bisho's erupted in bear hugs, hoots, handshakes, pecked cheeks and, for Johnny at least, palmed gifts of high-quality cocaine in one gram wraps. He declined the offer of a couple of escorts "on the ahse".

"Maybe later," said John. Ever gracious, ever the gent.

The feel of the club was as schizophrenic as Mad Jean Slater from *EastEnders* in blob week. The dance area doubled as a restaurant and was reasonably stylish, but the bar itself was like some 1970s nightmare of a pub, all dark wood, horse brasses and snapshot photographs of old faces – a celebration of a lost London, when the crime lords were home-grown and not imported from the wilder shores of Eastern Europe. It was a throwback that screamed out for spit and sawdust, and one which felt totally out of sync with the rest of the place.

It was a club where deals and fates alike were sealed, and here was I with my own personal devil, waiting for Lady Luck to blow on my dice or piss in my pocket.

We'd come "just for one" – one last late pint before the big night, instead we were now threatening to drink the joint dry. We sat at a corner table, next to the antique one-armed bandits, drinking bottled Stella with large whiskey chasers. No ice. It was going to get messy.

"This was a derelict lock-up until about eighteen months ago," said John.

"The bar's a bit..." I hesitated.

"Naff? Yeah, Bisho re-created the bar from his old pub."

"From the 70s?"

"No! 1996 – he never did have any taste."

"What are you going to do, John?"

"Drink, eat, fuck..."

"I mean long-term. After this is all done and dusted..."

"Play golf, do a bit of carp fishing..."

"What are you going to do for money?"

Baker grinned broadly. "You'll love this. They're going to turn my story into a movie. Stevie, my nephew, has had all the meetings already, the film has been priced up – £3mill – the money's in place, the director's signed up, we own the co-production company. I fancy Craig Fairbrass or Jason Statham playing me, but I'll make sure you're played by Danny Dyer so everyone will know from the start that you're the wrongun."

I looked at him. He was fucking serious. This had to be the cherry on top of the Heston Blumenthal supersized Bakewell tart of piss-taking that Baker was renowned for. And yet it made some kind of twisted sense, I suppose. The British public seem to have an endless appetite for gangster movies. We've already had *The Krays*, *Charlie*, *Sexy Beast*, *Layer Cake*, *Gangster Number One* and three movies made about Tucker and Tate, the Essex Boys...none as good as *Get Carter*. There were probably scores more, and at least the Baker brothers had been a bit more substantial than the made-up anti-heroes of any Guy Ritchie film you could mention.

British crime had long been overstuffed with two-bob wannabe Al Capones, parochial bully-boys, sadists and short-sighted psychopaths. John Baker was genuinely different. He was smart, at least as smart as Charlie Richardson, maybe smarter. Maybe history would see him the way he saw himself – as merely the blue-eyed poster boy for aggressive capitalism. A buccaneer, a prince of pirate enterprise...giving the people what they wanted, even if the law told them they couldn't have it. Breaking the rules, because the rules were wrong...

Garry Bushell

Where there was a demand, the Bakers had provided the supply. Everyone was happy – except the Law. And the little guys who got leaned on and hurt along the way.

All I said was, "So, finally you'll get your chance to go legit."

Johnny's big plan had always been to siphon the dirty money from the black market ops into legal earners and put serious distance between the core of the firm and what was going down at the street end; to make himself untouchable. He had been on the verge of pulling that off when I took him down.

John assembled a fat spliff using two Silk Cut Silvers. "You always knew that was the coup. But the world has changed since then. These days there are fellas getting cute around wind farms, picking up the fat EU grants along the way. It's sweet as a nut, definitely one up from the old VAT carousel scam. So we looked at that, and maybe we'll have a go. But this movie thing is even better, it's a proper 'up yours' to the Filth and we know we'll get the investment back on DVD sales alone. Here's to British justice. Cheers!"

For once I didn't have much to say.

"The way we treat entrepreneurs in this country is a joke," he said, scooping a handful of nuts off the neighbouring table. "It's like seeing rottweilers getting fucked by poodles. But this time the big bad devil dog is winning. I've got meself a nice bit of development land over Silvertown way – yeah, in scummy East London. Stevie has been worked hard. We've already got the planning permission for top-end flats for City boys. I'm meeting a literary agent bird next week too. She reckons she'll land me a £50K advance for an autobiography, and I'll be at the Hay Festival next summer amusing all those chinless cretins with weak handshakes and upper class gels called Jemima and Tabitha who have got the publishing industry sewn-up. Maybe I'll bag meself a couple before they go off shooting pheasants, or whatever they do when they're not spending Daddy's money, running comedy clubs or joining the Labour Party."

"Maybe you should do a cookbook after that, John, *How To Cook In Prison*. Like Paulie in *Goodfellas* slicing garlic, you know what I mean?"

"Are you hungry, gents?" asked a passing, fragrant blonde in her mid-50s.

"Only for your love, Nicola!"

116

"Soppy sod! Hold up, I'll get you the menu."

"Governor's wife," John said softly. "Had more renovation work done than Big Ben. Have a look."

Nicola came back from the bar with a small laminated list of unappetising culinary pleasures. Up close, her face did indeed carry the evidence of many futile cosmetic procedures. It had been pulled and peeled like a bucket of king prawns, and then poisoned, stretched, filled and prodded so much that it looked like she'd fallen asleep in a wind tunnel. A shame. Do people who have all this surgery done not realise we can tell? Look at poor old Dale Winton on the Lottery show, he can't even turn his head independently these days, he has to move his entire body instead.

"Fancy the meat madras?" I asked, my voice betraying a marked lack of enthusiasm.

"Only if they've found the vaccine for it."

"That bad?"

"You'd be better off with the cheese roll, hand stolen today from the Tesco dump bin."

"Oi you!" Nicola feigned hurt, although you couldn't tell from looking at her face.

John laughed. "Two of your finest cheese rolls please Nicki, easy on the pickle, there's a darling."

She went to get the grub.

"She must have turned a few heads in her time."

"Now it's just stomachs, mate."

Baker's smile evaporated. "You Harry, you actually had it worse than me – you were a prisoner with no release date. You must have felt like a deserter in 1944."

"That's true enough, John. Except I never deserted, the Old Bill deserted me."

He'd crumbled a liberal amount of opium into his spliff, making it a Buddha. "And you were on your Jack, of course. The wartime deserters had nowhere to go, so they ended up working with local gangs. In Paris towards the end of the war, there were so many AWOL tooled-up Yank servicemen it was like Chicago in 1929. I read a book about it. There were gun battles with the gendarme every fuckin' night...

"So you're living up north, hoping not to run into anyone who recognised you. No one to report to, no one to give you orders, an absolute lone wolf, nervous every time you went somewhere new. Oi, who's that at the bar? Some villain I stitched up. Some dirty slag of an undercover Old Bill. Some chinless MI5 wonder boy..."

"I got by, John, what can I say? I did what I had to do."

He sucked hard on his funny fag. "Must be tough being a spook these days. How do you do close surveillance? It ain't like the old days. You can't cut yerself a pair of eye-holes in your Kindle."

He was loving it. I changed the subject, allowing the dark cloud of my own doubts to drift across the habitual sunshine of his outlook.

"Do you trust them now? This deal they're offering?"

"About as much as you do. But let's say, like Jo Brand with a rape whistle, I'm optimistic. How about you? Worried?"

"More suspicious, like a man whose mail order Thai bride tells him he wants kids but insists on adopting."

He smiled. I could match him dodgy simile for dodgy simile all night long.

"How did you cope, John? Inside."

"I read. I read a lot. Dickens, Shaw, John Steinbeck, Sun Tzu. I found out about the stars, I studied them, studied the galaxy. If we were outside now, I could reel off the names of the constellations in the night sky like Patrick Moore on piece-rate....And I wrote, H. I wrote columns for the *Guardian* about criminal justice, I wrote the screenplay for this film..." he paused, perhaps surprised by his own seriousness. "You could be in it, Harry. We could always use a good tea-boy."

The bait was there, but I didn't rise to it.

"Did they ever give you psychiatric tests, John?"

"Yeah."

"I did 'em with some geezer from Reading University. He reckoned that if I'd been one point higher on the scale I would have been able to go into court and plead criminal insanity."

"Go on..."

"They had a few of us in, U/C officers. Did a whole load of other tests too. Under stress, they found that my heart rate actually slowed. Turns out that my anterior insular cortex, the part of my brain that governs empathy, and my amygdale – I think I said that right – the part that governs fear, are both 'significantly under-developed'."

"Which means you can use people, and you don't bottle it. Good warrior qualities. How many women did you bang in the course of undercover work?"

"I couldn't begin to add them all up."

"But if you laid 'em head to toe..."

"From here? I reckon we'd get to Mud Shute all right."

"Not for the first time." John chuckled, and then paused. Once again his smile dissolved. "I did think, while I was away, about how well you worked your way into us. You were like one of those Horse Stomach Bot bugs that hatch in a horse's mouth and chew through their tongue and burrow down right into their guts."

The hidden Hulk was showing his teeth. To deflate him, I went with it. "The art is to blend in, John. You don't want to be too loud, and draw too much attention to yourself. Get friendly with people on the fringes and work your way in. I had Lesley referencing me, and through her, Slobberin' Ron referencing me..."

"And through Ronald to me," he said thoughtfully. "Never too flash but amusing to be around. Good with a bit of banter. Being funny helps grease the passage..."

"So the world's leading sodomites say. But the job seriously fucks with your mind. You stop trusting everyone. You start acting the part even when you're at home."

"Losing the plot..."

"Oh yeah. I could have taken the time to sort out my home and family life, I should have, but you don't want to show any kind of weakness to your colleagues, it's damaging, you'd mug yourself off."

"And how did that make you feel?"

"Empty, and hollow..."

"Like the space between the stars," he said, quoting Raymond Chandler before switching tack. "We've got boys in the Met as well of course, the big players have. Oh I know you know about the odd bent cop but there's an actual network inside the Yard, it'll be a proper scandal if that story ever breaks. They've kept some proper A-team villains out of court for decades."

I nodded. I doubted that there was an actual network, but there would certainly be more than one detective in different areas taking bungs for tip-offs. Plenty of expensive high-profile criminal investigations had been abandoned because of leaks.

A sharp cry of pain to our left alerted us to a situation. A young kid, barely out of his teens, was on the floor, holding his ankle which was gushing blood. His Achilles tendon had been sliced, his Stanley knife had cluttered to the floor. We were both on our feet.

"Problem, Bisho?" John asked.

"Not now," muttered the governor in a voice as heavy and slow as the man himself.

Bisho was a short stocky guy who looked like Bob Hoskins re-imagined by Tolkien as a Hobbit. He moved like a 19th century convict dragging his chains, and spoke robotically in short staccato sentences, almost in monosyllables. "Li'l firm. Out of Camden Town. Trying to make a name for themselves. Slags. They won't come back."

He raised his voice. "All barred. Permanent. Got that?"

If there was anyone in the bar who didn't, they kept well quiet about it.

Time to lighten the mood.

"More beer?" I asked.

"Why not, bruv?"

There were a few people up the bar, including two quite striking Cockney birds, one blonde, one mixed race with a smile that would light up a mine shaft.

"Are you girls waiting to be served?" an ageing Romeo with yellow teeth asked them.

"No, we just like queuing," replied the blonde, deflating his swagger with such a neat twist of sarcasm it made me laugh out loud. We exchanged a little wink.

Bisho served me "on the ahse" ahead of the herd, and I took the drinks back to Johnny Too.

"Shall we get a couple of the girls over, just for company? There are some lookers at the bar."

"Go on then, better had, but only for their protection if it kicks off."

"Gotta be better than stumbling out of here nine sheets to the wind and picking up some bit of stray outside off the wet, heartless streets of Peckham, Fun City."

"True enough. Skinny bints. The Dorises round here give you a blow-job just to get something warm inside them...You can have the one that looks like a Klingon in a wig, mind."

"Klingon?"

"I bet she does."

"Ta-da!"

"If you were captured by aliens would you rather they keep you in their zoo or their circus?"

"Zoo. All the grub, none of the graft."

"For me it'd be the circus every time. The zoo would be too much like doing bird. In the circus, you've got more chance of escaping – or at least taking a few of them out with you."

"Like they'd ever give you access to the cannon."

I called out to the bar. "GIRLS! Fancy joining us?"

They started to walk over. "I'll have Miss Dynamite, yours is the blonde in the big heels who looks like Mollie King from the Saturdays, right?"

"Yeah, she looks at least 98 per cent Chlamydia free...And no sign of an Adam's apple."

"Ha. She ain't my type, John."

"Tsk. All them years undercover, I had you down as a better liar than that."

49

Paddock Wood, Kent. Five hours later

Gary Shaw's radio alarm woke him up in time for the 7am Radio 4 Today Show news. It took a moment for the words to filter through the early morning mind-fuzz. The headline story concerned a suspected terrorist device that had detonated in the West End in the early hours, leaving a young man critically injured.

Instinctively, Shaw knew that this was connected to his case. He was right.

50

Temple, London EC4, three hours later

I had another meeting with an ice cream from Box 500 at my barrister's office just off Middle Temple Lane. He was a good man, Mark Wyatt, a QC into his Chelsea and his Ska. I wanted expert guidance and he was the best. You need someone shit hot on your team, especially when you wake up to find that the Tasmanian Devil has taken residence in your cerebral cortex, and that the bastard has decided to take up drumming.

There were no problems with the agreement we signed. I can't say too much about it – Official Secrets and all that. But Mark reckoned it was as cast iron as it could be, in the circumstances, with the funny firm involved. What it meant, in simple terms, was that once this job was done I would be a free and upright citizen once again. The past would be re-written with a Stalinist zeal. Ireland would be wiped from the records, as would the file about my suspected involvement in the Nelson killings. I did ask if that meant I'd get me police pension. The geezer from Thames House said he'd get back to me. I won't hold me breath.

I had a quick breakfast beer with Mark, then shot off to buy some party clobber. I'd travelled down light, just one change of clothes and my emergency grab bag containing the usual – false passports, bundles of cash (pounds and Euros), Sexton Blake credit cards, condoms, painkillers, amphetamine, hair dye, hand gun (a Glock 21) and ammo. A proper little Jason Bourne I was, mate, ready for anything, fight, flight or fuck, at any time

51

Tonbridge, Kent.

Grim-faced Gary Shaw assembled his team. The London bomb was the talk of the office. Especially now that the unfortunate clubber Dom Wilson had died from his injuries. Pictures of the victim in happy times wearing an Aqua Plaid short sleeved shirt had now appeared on the *London Evening Standard* website.

"So it's true," remarked Womble. "Dead men do wear plaid."

The joke stank like the detective's breath; Gary Shaw ignored it. "You know what this means, don't you?"

"SO15?" suggested DC Woodward.

"Yep, they will be all over this now like a cheap suit. We'll be taken off the case, which means if we want to wrap this up ourselves we have to get a result tonight."

"Guv," Wattsie said slowly.

"Yeah?"

"Now that there is no reasonable doubt that Broadwick's column is the catalyst inspiring these crimes, don't you think someone needs to have a word? He wrote about 'putting a bomb under the EU' and this has happened. There's a big difference between a set of coincidences and a recognisable pattern. He needs to be made aware that a madman is taking what he writes literally, extremely literally."

Shaw surveyed their wall full of pin boards detailing every incident. Every case, every picture was linked to a piece by William Broadwick.

"Yes. I need to bat this upstairs, but he'll have to be told."

52

Tunbridge Wells, Kent. 1.30pm

Victor Oswald Stevens had been a local legend. He'd won the George Medal in Aden with the 2nd Battalion Coldstream Guards in 1964 when Gulliver was thirteen, fighting the Egyptian-backed NLF, or "sand niggers" as he'd always called them. He also served with distinction in Mauritius. Gulliver looked at his late brother's medal, displayed next to his picture in his living room, and wept, as he'd seen Victor do for the first and only time when his own schoolboy pal Bernie had died saving the lives of his SAS comrades in Borneo. Pancreatic cancer had taken Vic quickly eighteen months ago. Within three months of the cancerous cells being discovered, Victor Stevens was dead. It was one battle the old soldier couldn't win.

Gulliver – 'Gully', Vic had called him – bit his lip and fought back more tears. His brother had been his rock when they were kids, five years old with the strength and balls to stand up to their violent, alcoholic father. In 1974, Victor had introduced his younger sibling to General Sir Walter Walker, whose anti-Communist politics subsequently shaped both of their world views. Walter Walker had envisaged a time when the army might take over Britain, to the acclaim of the public who "might choose rule by the gun in preference to anarchy". Both brothers had joined the Unison group, which existed to supply volunteers in event of a long threatened re-run of the 1926 general strike. Mercifully, the election of the sainted Margaret in 1979 had consigned fears of Red revolution to the dustbin of history for a generation.

What would the General make of the country now? What would Victor? We betrayed their memory by doing nothing. He owed it to these brave, fearless men to fight for what was right by whatever means possible.

The knock that Gulliver was waiting for came. He opened the door to the two young men from the British Freedom Party, looking uncomfortable in the wedding suits they had chosen to wear. Stevens had invited them round to collect a cash donation. They stayed for tea and biscuits. The conversation ranged from immigration to the traveller blight via the insight and popular appeal of William Broadwick. Gulliver spoke with such clarity and conviction that they had ended up asking the farmer if he'd stand for them at the European elections in 2015. They also invited him and a guest to the coming London rally. Gulliver Stevens readily agreed, and offered to bring his "very bright, very organised, very committed" daughter along to help out behind the scenes. He had good days and bad days. Today had been a good day. Tonight, he was sure, would be even better.

53

7pm Stringfellows, London, West End

I got down to Stringies early to case the joint and meet up with Gary Shaw, who gave me a guided tour of what was what and who'd be where. It was a big operation. He had plain clothes all over the gaff, even a cute little red-head behind the bar who turned out to be a detective sergeant and who could read me my rights any time the mood took her.

"And you're sure he'll show?" I asked.

"Odds on, Harry. The creep has been following Broadwick's column like the guy is Moses publishing the Commandments on a twice weekly basis..."

"Monkey read, monkey do."

"Something like that."

I had a quick half, Shaw declined. He told me about the bomb. "Which is why we've got to nab him tonight," he said, looking grave.

"This bloke isn't a little cracked, is he Gary? He's totally gone, a man on a mission. We're stepping in front of an oncoming express train for you, mate."

"I know, and tonight we'll derail it."

Or die trying, I thought.

"How is the job now, Gal?"

"The same as it always was, too many chiefs and not enough Indians. It's all about statistics now and intelligence dissemination. To be honest, the copper on the street has not got a clue what's really going on. It's one cock-up after another."

"Nine o'clock you want us here?"

"Yes please."

I downed my lager and went to get John.

***

We made our grand red carpet entrance at nine on the dot, emerging out of a bullet-proof limo to a sea of paparazzi and TV cameras. Let the hounds see the fox...

Out of necessity, I had dressed quite plainly: simple black Armani T-shirt, navy blazer, dark denim jeans, brown Sendra ankle boots; but somehow Johnny had managed to get hold of a classy Tom Ford three-piece suit which probably retailed at

Garry Bushell

over £2K. He looked flasher than a Russian oligarch on the pull, and as sharp as the blade he had no doubt got concealed in the pocket of his strides.

There had been talk of demonstrations outside, but the threat of counter-marches had persuaded the Home Secretary to ban demos within a one mile radius of the club. Instead, a token protest of just twelve people had been allowed. They were middle-aged 'Broadies' (the tabloid term for William Broadwick supporters), holding placards with slogans such as 'What about the victims?', 'Bring back the rope' and 'Baker Back In Jail'.

Inside, the club was buzzing. Mod DJ Paul Hallam played 'What's Wrong With Me, Baby?' by the Invitations as security ushered us to the VIP enclosure past a pop-up stall serving free pie and mash – in honour of South London's prodigal son. Above our heads were nets heavy with blue and white Millwall FC party balloons, and pride of place in the VIP section was a provocative ice sculpture of a handgun and silencer.

Genial Peter Stringfellow himself welcomed us to our seats. My eyes were everywhere. The place was full of South London's criminal elite, the extended Baker family "as staunch as the Home Guard" according to Johnny, Soho faces, minor name pop singers, fame chasing models and sympathetic soap stars. There was also, I noticed, a party of hired-in lookalikes: a Keith Lemon, an Adele, a great Del-Boy Trotter, a decent Liz Hurley, a rather poor Tony Curtis in a skimpy toga, one extra-large Mr T and two Nicki Minajs.

"Nice. I wouldn't mind a Minaj a trois," I remarked to John. "Here, is that the real Joey Essex?"

"Who gives a monkey's toss?"

"Good point."

"That is the real Harry May, though."

I followed his line of vision and saw the wizened visage of a legendary old South London villain, once known optimistically as 'the Robin Hood of SE1'. It was half right, May definitely took from the rich...

The two men exchanged thumbs up, which John followed with a clenched fist salute of solidarity.

A Richard appeared at my side, her hand went straight to my thigh as she whispered exhausting sounding promises into my shell-like. I liked the Bermondsey accent and the mandarin and orange blossom whiff of her Coco Chanel eau de parfum, but she looked a bit too much like Mario Balotelli's idea of a classy bird, you know what I mean? All fake tits, hair the colour of stale piss, and a dress that barely covered her costs. "I want to taste you," she murmured, in a voice heavy with promise. I smiled and said I'd see her later. Well, you never know how the night's going to end up.

John was on his feet kissing another woman.

"H, this is Maxine," he said. "My future ex-wife. Max, this is Harry, he used to be filth but now he's just West Ham scum."

"Lovely to meet you, Max," I said, pecking her cheek. "Thanks, John. Do you want to take your knife, or just leave it stuck in me back?"

He roared and gave me a bear hug. I felt the pressure of the gun that was in a shoulder holster carefully concealed under his jacket – unauthorised, naturally. I was packing too, and ditto.

"What is this classy lady doing with a bloke like you?" I smiled, winking at her.

"Everything you fuckin' dream about, mate," he replied.

Hallam played 'Soul Drummers' by Ray Barretto. What a groove. Pure class. One by one, a procession of villainous faces came up to pay their respects. One retired North London Peterman, Jack Vance, well into his late sixties turned up with a Britney Spears doppelganger on his arm. The girl could have been anything between seventeen and a fifteen month stretch. The necklace she was wearing probably cost more than my car.

"Fuck me, Jack, is it 'bring your daughter to work' day?" cracked Johnny. The old fella's lip curled like one of Ali Baba's slippers, but he forced a smile and said nothing. "Hope you've stocked up on Fisher Price condoms."John switched his attention to the girl. "Oi, Lolita, you seen this watch, luv?" John flashed a top-end Rolex. "I got it today from a bloke down Deptford market...£15 grand..."

The gag soared over her pretty peroxide head like the Red Arrows, but Baker was in his element, he'd be reeling them in all night. It must seem odd to some, I guess, to see this powerful alpha male conceal his obvious intelligence behind a barrage of coarse wisecracks but that was his shtick, his shield, his modus operandi. The jolly hardcase. The killer clown. And I was the same. It was how we were brought up, using one-liners as weapons. It was a banter culture that grew out of growing up in hard places. You had to laugh or else you'd cry. Soldiers, firemen, medics, cops too...we all relied on that dark humour to stay sane. Even to this day, I'd rather listen to Bernard Manning ripping the piss out of a party of saps than some smart-arse graduate being 'ironic'.

Stringfellow conjured up medium-rare steaks and a medium-bare lap-dancer with a lion tattoo on her thigh started to do her stuff – how many times had she had to suffer 'big pussy' cracks on account of that naff old bit of ink?

Peter's stunning brunette wife Bella was chatting away to Maxine Slater. "We're trying for a baby," he told me proudly.

"I don't blame you mate, if she was my missus we'd be trying for a baby every night and twice on Sundays."

The club owner laughed and started chatting to Ronnie Wood – the real one, I think. Gary Shaw appeared at my side, with another copper in disguise. Some people just shouldn't be CID. This guy was fat, we're talking Greggs on legs, and so shifty he looked like he'd just robbed a post office and was looking for somewhere to dump his mask.

"All okay, Gal?"

"Yeah, except for me sciatica kicking in. You?"

"No problem. I'm on bottled water now. Head as clear as your bank account. Anything suspicious yet?"

"Not yet. But security has been kept deliberately loose. We want this character to be able to weasel his way past the doormen."

"It's still early. Plenty of time..."

"You see the Jack the Ripper?" asked his pal, the shifty-looking cop. The bloke had breath like a freshly exhumed corpse.

I nodded, handing him a piece of gum.

"I could pull a stretch for what I'm thinking."

"Ha ha. Save it for Her Indoors mate."

"If I did that it'd get rusty."

Can't say I blame her, I thought. Peter Stringfellow threw his arm around his shoulder, and recoiled slightly from the quick blast of badger breath.

"Enjoying yourself lads?"

"It's the 'feminism for beginners' class, Peter?" I replied.

"We're just admiring your stripper," Shaw's pal said.

"They're not strippers," the club-owner said, looking hurt. "We don't have strippers. We have entertainers, dancers. End of story."

"Quite right," I said. "You should sue them for defamation. Get yer writs out for the lads..."

The club owner grimaced, while the chastised cops left us to mingle awkwardly with genuine party goers. Gary walked off like a penguin with cramp. I noticed that his colleague kept checking his wallet, probably sensible. There were more dippers here than Oxford Street.

Strippers, lap-dancers, performance 'artistes' – call them what you will, they never had much appeal to me. If I wanted to mix with unhappy birds who hated my guts but wanted my money, women who were happy to turn me on and then leave me harder than a Cyberman's helmet, I'd just go drinking over Chelsea way with a load of Sloanes.

I sat and watched the next batch of party guests arrive. They were an odd mix: hulking great geezers from Eastern Europe who looked like they'd just walked in from a Grimms fairy tale, a skinny once-famous ex-model whose boat, due to ill-advised cosmetic surgery, now resembled a tightly squeezed toothpaste tube, a couple of heavy Malts, and a statuesque former soap actress, her handsome face partially eroded by too much Marbella sun, who still looked the business.

"She's hot in France," said a passing snapper who had followed my gaze.

"Yeah? So was Joan of Arc, mate."

Johnny Too was having an animated conversation with a silver-haired fox involving the words 'graft' and 'nose-bag'. Not to be sniffed at, they say... My moby buzzed. It was a text from Knockers. She was coming down to London with her dad tomorrow morning for some rally and would I meet her for dinner? I texted back a smiley face and turned off the phone. I wasn't in the mood to start playing text ping-pong right now. In fact, I had started to feel a little anxious. I got up to stretch me legs and have a quick nose about, get my own 'wrong'un radar' working overtime.

The celebrity table next to ours had filled up nicely. There was Barbara Windsor, laughing and clucking, Wilf Pine, the only Englishman to have become a 'made man' in the Gambino crime family, talk radio jocks Nick Ferrari and James Whale, ancient showbiz hack Rick Sky looking the same age now as he had done in the 80s, a definite mirror in the attic job that one, Chris Quentin, formerly from *Coronation Street* – a long time formerly – and some woman with a great smile who I recognised as an ITV weathergirl but couldn't place her name. Quite a looker. We're talking about warm front leading to mounting high pressure in the trouser area. Beyond them were a table of porn stars familiar to students of that dubious art form under the noms du plumes – noms du plunge? –of Trixie Merriman, Rebel Knight and Brian 'Big-below' Belton.

I recognised the geezers with them as Kev 'The Hammer' Moody, and Si 'Spanner' Sternchuss and wondered if all the other porn barons had nicknames drawn from the toolbox. Come on down Sid Screwdriver, Chico Chisel and Willie Wrench...The shit that goes through your mind when you're killing time...

The red-head detective sergeant behind the bar caught my eye. I gave her a little wink. She winked back. Oh yeah. On a normal night she'd be in with a chance. She still might be. No way was I going home alone tonight.

54

The Nell Gwynne Tavern, London, The Strand

The great reunion had turned out to be as tedious as William Broadwick had expected. He didn't like the scruffy, no-frills pub, with its dim lighting, Estonian bar staff, its lack of any food option that wasn't served between slices of corner shop bread and the absence of anything remotely approaching a decent wine. On the plus side, they had Bombardier on tap and at least he didn't have to struggle to hear what anyone else was saying. There must be louder morgues.

Broadwick sank three pints of premium lager in rapid succession. All of his old school friends had turned up, with their wives, a dismal bunch of loud under-educated women. It was good to see them all though: Pete McDermid, Al Chandler, Chris Billingham...even Paul Leather, who he didn't really get on with. There was something pleasing about the mix of easy nostalgia and absolute trust that springs from knowing someone for half a life-time.

The talk was of families, jobs, and then inevitably for the men, football and politics. The unfulfilled dreams would come many pints later. Slowly, as always happened, the group divided along gender lines, the women to the right of the bar. The men re-assembling to the left, gathering around the soundless TV tuned to Sky Sports, as much for the additional lighting as the indifferent match.

Paul Leather, usually so hostile because of the chasm between their politics, seemed particularly friendly. The two men ended up sitting on a corner table, where Paul was happy to discreetly share the decent brandy he'd smuggled in his bag. He topped William up whenever the grumpy, twenty-something bar manager wasn't looking.

"Are you still a Red, Leather?" Broadwick asked looking for a fight.

"After Blair and Brown who could be?" came the reply he wasn't expecting. "Thirteen years of a Labour Prime Minister and the working man is right back at the bottom of the pile. The few of us who can actually find work, that is..."

"The ones who haven't been undercut by imported labour force, legal and illegal," Broadwick nodded.

"And the NHS has turned shittier than a freshly used bed-pan..."

"We're in love with the myth of it but run scared of the shocking reality."

"That's true enough, I suppose. But of course the Tories are no better. I still believe in progress, Will. I just can't find a party that suits the way I feel."

"What do you mean by progress?"

"Change of course, change for the better."

"And do you see this progress anywhere? In any aspect of our culture, in education or in art or in our standard of living?"

The words came with a sneer worthy of Paxman with the hump.

"Only in culture, I suppose."

"Really? I'd like to know where Paul, because all I can see in Western culture is a steady, continued erosion."

"Music...comedy..."

"Are you joking? Modern comedians are is a bunch of overpaid, over-privileged brats relying on smut for easy, forgettable laughs! And these preening fools are taken seriously by our liberal Left establishment and feted with guest spots on *Question Time*, for God's sake."

"Well our rock music is still good."

"Who?"

"Well, I guess Coldplay..."

"Are you really suggesting Chris Martin can hold a candle to Keith Emerson?"

Paul topped up his glass.

"Even the bands we used to listen to and love, Pink Floyd, Genesis, ELP, Yes, King Crimson, you can't seriously suggest they're in the same ball park as Vaughan Williams or Benjamin Britten, let alone Bach, Wagner, Beethoven and the rest. I listen to One Direction and all I hear is a ringing cash register..."

"Hey, Will mate, I don't think they're aiming at you."

"No, but tell me one great 'pop' act ever that deserves to be treated seriously. Bob Dylan and his doggerel?

John Lennon singing 'imagine no possessions' on a £1million piano?

It's laughable."

"Lennon wrote, or co-wrote some of the greatest popular music ever made."

"Ever made? Or of his generation? Gilbert wrote wittier words, Sullivan came up with superior tunes, as did Richard Rodgers and Jerome Kern. And let's not even start on all the crap John Lennon endorsed – Yippies, Trots, suspect Maharishis, callous IRA murderers, Michael X, another bloody murderer... Compare Lennon's lyrics to Hart or Porter, he can't touch them. He doesn't come close to Johnny Mercer..."

"I've never heard of Johnny Mercer. But my point is I'd still rather listen to 'Norwegian Wood' than anything from a West End musical, and I'd rather listen to the Allman Brothers than any opera you could name. Complex doesn't necessarily mean better, in my humble opinion."

"No, and there is plenty of folk and choral music that I adore, but looking at the big picture what we have is a rush of Gadarene swine to the lowest common denominator. You see a supposed intellectual like Alan 'Two Jobs' Yentob praised for fawning over washed-up pop has-beens. To me it's just a sign of our infantilised society. It's a virus, and it's spread right across the board. Plays, art, poetry, literature – all of them are shot, all of them inferior, all crippled by the curse of modernity, the culturati's love affair with crap. There hasn't been a decent novel written in our lifetime."

"Woah, that's a big claim. You were born in 1957, same year as me, so there have been loads of acclaimed classics since then. Let's think, *Portnoy's Complaint*?"

"Wank! Literally wank! All the books that figure in those preposterous lists of great modern novels you occasionally find in the *Sunday Times* or the *Observer* are irredeemably inferior to the best that have gone before. I saw Rushdie's *Midnight's Children* listed in the *Guardian*, it's virtually unreadable."

"*The Bonfire Of The Vanities*?"

"Yes, that's good."

"Got you there, then!"

"No, I said it was good. I didn't say it was a classic. It's been a long time since Steinbeck, Wodehouse and Orwell."

"And you hate modern art too?"

"What is there to like about it? Seriously, Paul. Damien Hirst is a conman, Gormley's work is ugly...Saatchi paid £150,000 for an unmade bed! Cows cut in half, a tiger shark in a tank, lights going on and off...and this crap is elevated to the level of Rembrandt? Give me strength! It's been the Emperor's New

Clothes since day one, an absolute racket. These trend-chasing mug punters can't even see they're being hustled."

"You know, you may have a point. But who's to blame?"

"You know as well as I do."

"What do you mean?"

Broadwick lowered his voice. "Look at the religious background of the people who push this tripe the most ardently..."

"Are you saying what I think you're saying?"

Broadwick lowered his voice even more, Paul leaned in closer. "It's Jewish hustlers all the way down the line, and we're the schmucks who fell for it."

Paul thought this was blatantly absurd. He had been obsessed with top-flight Jewish humour for years, everyone from Woody Allen to Larry David via Mort Sahl, Seinfeld and Jackie Mason, and had read every word Marx, Engels and Lev Bronstein had ever written. But he was content, in fact delighted, for now, to let Broadwick ramble on.

"They aren't a creative people. They're users, exploiters, the cultural equivalent of the teredo shipworm."

"I'm not sure about that, I'm not comfortable with anti-Semitism."

"I'm not an anti-Semite, just look at who the champions of the anti-culture are and draw your own conclusions. These are facts, suppressed facts, but facts all the same. Think about it. There are no great Jewish composers or authors or original thinkers."

"Duh, not even Einstein?"

"Duh, no! He was a plagiarist, just like your blessed Marx was!"

Paul shifted uncomfortably. "I need a fag. Can you get us a lager top Willie, please?"

Five minutes later, they both stoodin Bull Inn Court, the alley outside the pub.

"How have you been since the divorce?" asked William with mock concern. The slur on 'since' told Paul Leather that the brandy had achieved the desired effect.

"Not too bad, thanks. Losing my job hurt more, but the good times in the television game are over. Luckily I had some money put away for a rainy day, I just wasn't expecting a monsoon..."

He took a drag on his fag. "I'm seeing someone else now," he confided, raising the stakes. "She's a teacher, 32. Bangs like a shit-house door."

"Tell me about it! I've got one that wears me out."

"You mean, you're over the side?" The $64million question.

"Like a liferaft! Don't tell the others will you?"

Ker-ching! "Of course not."

"Jackie. A little beauty, works for Cameron. Knows I'm married and doesn't care."

"Works for Cameron? *The* Cameron? David Cameron?"

"Yes, but not directly. Her firm handles their public relations guff."

Ker-ching! Ker-ching! "Decent bunk-up?"

"God, yes. The best I've ever had, and so up for it I can't tell you. We've done things that before I'd only read about. Positions, places..."

"Cars?"

"Car backseats, bushes, laybys, hotels, stables. Handcuffs, S&M, spoons...it's like she's using *Fifty Shades* is her starter manual...and that's another rotten book by the way."

"And Fiona?"

"Has no idea."

"How long?"

"Oh well over a year..."

A less self-absorbed man might have noticed the almost imperceptible smile that had crept over Paul Leather's face.

"I'll be thinking of you as Christian Grey from now on," he said. "Or Christian Grave when I see you try to out-grump Hitchens on *Question Time*. I'd settle for the Rumpo Kid myself! Come on, they'll start sending out search parties for us soon and it gives me the creeps out here. It's supposed to be haunted isn't it?"

"Oh yes, famously. They say a stage hand from the Adelphi murdered an actor called William Terris in this very back alley back in Victorian times – I suppose reviewers were tougher back then! It's said that his tormented spirit still haunts the area where we're standing."

"Another good reason to go back in."

"Agreed, come on, I'm starting to get a sense of impending doom."

Paul Leather grinned. The fat Tory prick didn't know the half of it.

55

Midnight, Stringfellows.

Minutes of nothing happening turned to hours of nothing happening. Maxine and Bella had gone off dancing; Johnny who had been filling his boots with free shampoo had been deep in a relatively sensible conversation with a classy brunette on the subject of penal reform, but was now discussing the effect the US craft brewing explosion had had on micro-distillers. Full of surprises, our John.

The woman was quite exquisite too, a bit like a taller Audrey Tautou but not quite as painfully undernourished. I caught Gary Shaw's eye and motioned that I was going for a quick gypsy's. En route, the cut-price Bermondsey Bardot pulled me to one side.

"So, are you taking me home handsome, or what?"

"I'll take you as far as my hotel room, if you like."

"Oh, I like."

Bang on! "I'd better warn you, though, tomorrow morning I probably won't remember your name."

"Darling, after what I'm going to do to you, you won't remember your own name."

Get in! I laughed. "Just popping to the little boys' room..."

"Not that little I hope..."

"Ha. No. Trust me, it'll fill a pram. I'll collect you on the way through, okay?"

She smiled and pinched my arse. Feisty girl, and nicely curvy – I have no interest in women who look like size zero fetish models – but something told me I wouldn't want to listen to this one's iPod.

So what had happened to our bold vigilante? Clearly, something must have spooked him. Maybe he sniffed this out as a set-up. Maybe he was laying low. Who knew? It did look like we were going to make our own fun tonight though.

The other two geezers in the khazi were only there for a bit of what the degenerate youth of today call 'ream nose-bag', so I was in and out like an SAS raid. I can't have been gone more than three minutes but when I came back to the sound of Darrow Fletcher's 'Pain Gets A Little Deeper', a massive great ruck had broken out between the lookalikes and a group of hounds from Deptford. It was like a proper bar-room brawl from a Western. Furniture was being flung, glasses smashed, geezers in penguin suits were getting stuck into each other, while women gibbered like a bunch of laboratory monkeys. Was this a good time to mention Health and Safety?

I couldn't help grinning as the Keith Lemon lookalike got a paper plate full of pie and mash slap bang in the mooey; it would have been even funnier if the pie had been a custard one. And a lot riskier if Mr T had been on the receiving end...I pity the food...

One of the Minaj lookalikes was using her stiletto heel like an actual stiletto, jabbing it into a fat bird's fleshy neck. The Tony Curtis recoiled, accidentally stepped on some big lump's toes, and was sent sprawling. He landed in the most painful way imaginable on the ice sculptured hand-gun, the barrel of which, combined with the silencer, was at least nine inches in length with a four inch girth. Curtis didn't get that in *The Rawhide Years*...

Gents, if you need a reason why not to wear a toga and no underpants to a party, look no further. Tony's scream would have brought a tear to a glass eye.

To add another layer of unexpected farce, the drunk and distracted DJ mistook his agonised yelping as a cue to release the Millwall balloons from their netting. That's the best way to see their colours – going down.

Gary Shaw and his battalion of stealth Old Bill went into action...it's a shame his shifty-looking oppo didn't just sling his trap wide open. The bloke must personally generate 55 per cent of the country's supply of halitosis. But as it happened, the fight was over as quickly as it had begun. Just a tanked-up tear-up, nothing more, nothing to worry about. Still Johnny must be loving this – he did say he wanted to end up in a circus.

As the warring parties were separated, I looked over to our table. No Johnny Too. I scanned the room quickly, only to catch the sight of John disappearing out of the front door with the brunette, Audrey Too-Tall. For fuck's sake. I started after them, but it wasn't easy getting through the throng. I'm not as fit or as fast as I was.

56

The NCP car park, Upper St Martin's Lane

Johnny had no idea who this woman was, and neither did he care. All that mattered was she was cute, sexy and apparently up for a quick bout of sexual Tasering. He'd steered the conversation away from sloe gin to slow comfortable screws, and she'd responded by saying how important the *root* was to the taste of gin. She'd mentioned angelica root and orris root, and then, her hand slipping between his legs, the possibility of some quick rooting in the relative safety of the NCP.

By the look of her he'd expected to find she drove a Chelsea tractor, but the girl, called Lotte, had taken him to the back of a clapped out Ford Transit van. Johnny Baker laughed.

"What the fuck's this? Ha! Are we going dogging, love? It looks like a fuckin' kidnapper's van? Ha-ha. Take me I'm yours, I'll go eas..."

CRACK!

"As easily as that," she said softly.

***

"You seen, John?"

The big lug on the door was either dumb, deaf or pig ignorant.

I grabbed his lapels. "Johnny Baker. It's his party. He just left. With a brown-haired girl. Which way did they go?"

The doorman put one hand on my shoulder and went to clump me with the other one. I kneed the soppy cunt straight in the nuts – the orchestras, we call them, although in his case the brass section was entirely between his ears. His hands went down to briefly cradle his bruised bollocks and then turned into granite fists.

He was bigger than me, about fifteen stone – fourteen without his aftershave. But before he could recover, I put him on his back with a snappy three punch combination: right, left, right...bosh. Over and out. You never lose it.

"Who saw John Baker leave here with a brunette, minutes ago?"

"They disappeared into the car park," shouted a helpful paparazzo between snaps.

"Ta."

I did wonder briefly why he hadn't chased after them, but then Johnny growling at you would discourage all but the boldest smudger. The car park eh? Sweet, he'd probably poggering the granny out of that little sort in the back of her jamjar by now. But he still needed me to watch his back, figuratively I meant. I didn't actually want to watch them at it. I'm not Dave Courtney.

I reached the second floor in time to see the brunette shutting the back of a Transit van. Baker was nowhere in sight. Alarm bells rang. Something told me this mystery woman was a mantrap in mascara.

"Oi!"

She looked up and appeared momentarily worried, but quickly recovered her composure. My piece was in my hand.

"Where's Johnny, luv?"

"He's gone. He said I was to meet him at his hotel. I've just come for my overnight bag."

Of course he did. This stank like a mermaid brothel when the tide's gone out.

"So where is it?"

"What?"

"The bag."

She hesitated.

"Open the doors; I want a look in that van. Now!"

She did as she was told, but slowly. I motioned her to stand back with the business end of the Glock. I could see a pair of finely suited legs inside, which naturally belonged to the now unconscious John Baker. The drunken sap had obviously fallen for her hook, line and plonker.

"Okay. Don't move." I went for my phone with my free hand, but never reached it.

When I came round, many hours later, I realised that she must have had an accomplice. Of course she fuckin' had. Whoever it was had done me good and proper from behind.

57

Tonbridge, Kent

Mick Neale had taken Thelma out to a restaurant. She'd been impressed by the decor, and the menu, which was such a shoddy work of fiction it should have had 'by Jeffrey Archer' on the front of it. The important thing though was he'd managed to stay sober. They kissed outside her house, tenderly at first but then more urgently. She invited him in "for coffee" and he settled down in the living room, readying himself for the next part of the dating ritual. He wasn't great with the flirtatious small talk, but then neither it appeared was Thelma, who came back from the kitchen with neither coffee nor clothes...

They used to say there were a million stories in the naked city; Mick Neale had finally found one to match.

***

Mick woke up at 3am, in her bed, unable to get back to sleep, and unwilling to move in case he disturbed her. He listened to her breathing for a while and then let his mind wander. He'd heard a report on the London bomb in the car coming over. TalkSPORT had an expert on who had explained how easy these home-made devices were to construct with the right blend of chemicals. Something about them sounded familiar, and now, in the middle of the night, he realised why. He'd seen all of them recently, in the Stevens barn.

Thelma stirred and put her hand on his chest.

"You awake?" she whispered.

"Yeah."

Her hand slid slowly south. Mick's erection was so quick it almost came with a cartoon sound effect.

58

Saturday, 10am. The City Of London.

William Broadwick had been summoned to the Express offices in Lower Thames Street by his Editor. The last time that happened he got a pay rise and a TV series. This time, he was due to meet a DI Shaw, but in his place some fellow called Woodward with a face like a seaside Punch had turned up.

The detective apologised for his governor's absence, and cut to the chase. The PowerPoint display left little room for doubt. Broadwick's face fell as the link between his columns and the spate of vigilante crimes were inexorably underlined, and then he winced as he realised that early on he'd actually approved of the scumbag's actions, actions which had become increasingly unpredictable and unhinged. William hadn't felt well to begin with, but as Woodward's display finished, he threw up all over the Editor's expensive shag pile carpet.

59

Surrey, moments later.

Jackie Sutton saw Bang Bang Kirpachi's name flashing on her mobile phone and took the call eagerly.

"Have you seen him yet?" she asked anxiously.

"Oh yeah. I'm just leaving South London now."

"Did it go to plan?"

"Better than we'd ever imagined. We've got the quotes to stand up your torrid affair 100 per cent, and we've got something much nastier, should you ever need it."

"Really? What?"

"Rampant career-killing anti-Semitism."

"Ouch!"

"So what do I do now?"

"Proceed with part one of the plan. Confirm a figure with the *Mail* as soon as."

"Pictures and taped quotes now..."

"Yes, so you'll get five figures easily."

"Sweet, my love, sweet as a honey-coated nut."

"Is Paul happy?"

"Over the moon. I gave him a monkey, and his face lit up like a kid at Christmas. The only thing he said was 'Take the fat little Nazi bastard down'."

"He's not fat! He's cuddly. But you've got the microcassette, yeah?"

"Oh yeah. It's all yours."

"Great. Only play them the relevant quotes, don't let them keep it. The only thing we're taking down today is his sham of a marriage."

60

Tonbridge, Kent

It's dark. No light, no windows. My head aches, my back aches, there's a gag in my mouth, my hands are tied and I need a piss. Actually I lied when I said my head aches. This is no ache, it's more a throb and not a regular hangover throb either. I was used to them. No, this throb is a lurching, jerking, unpredictable stabbing pain. I reach up and touch the back of my head, and feel the dampness of recently spilled blood and a bump that could get me dates with unicorns.

Just my luck. I'd planned on spending last night in the Dorchester, I should have been coming a lot in that aerobic Bardot doll, not coming to in a claustrophobic coal hole. I strain my eyes against the gloom. I can see Johnny Too still out cold to my left, and a few feet in front of me, at the top of eight or nine steps, the outline of a door. I start to roll towards the stairs and realise my foot is chained up. Hmm. How do you get room service in a joint like this?

61

The news of Johnny Too's abduction was all over the London editions of every national newspaper, along with talk of a second man being taken and much speculation about who might be behind the crime. All of the mystery was blown away at midday when a phone call to the Press Association alerted the watching world to a video that had been posted on YouTube.

Gary Shaw groaned as he watched it on Sky News. The footage showed John Baker and Harry Tyler bound, gagged and unconscious in a dark, bare room with brick walls while a man in a balaclava talking through a voice distorter spoke of the need for society to avenge itself on those who flaunt the Law, and the alien forces that allow them to do so.

A detailed statement issued later listed those forces as weak liberal judges, pansy pink lawyers, the 'gauleiters' of the European courts, and traitor politicians, many of whom were named. It was signed on behalf of the English Liberation Front by Judge Hopssen.

Shaw was straight on the phone to Rhona Watts. "Wattsie, what's this 'Judge Hopssen' thing? Another piss-take name?"

"Give me five guv," replied the sergeant.

She actually rang back twelve minutes later.

"It's worse than before, guv. This one is Joseph Sugden."

"Enlighten me."

"Joe Sugden, Emmerdale. The soap opera. He was a farmer in it."

Shaw shook his head. "For fuck's sake! They're laughing at us."

"So what now?"

"For us, nothing. They've taken it off us, it's been kicked upstairs. We fucked up."

62

Tonbridge, Kent.

The room smelt of something. Maybe rats, I wasn't sure. Definitely some kind of animals. I heard Johnny start to stir. I stood up and started stamping, making as much commotion as I could.

The door ahead started to rattle.

"Pack that in!" An old bastard with bat ears in a lumberjack shirt came down the stairs carrying a plate of sandwiches in one hand, and a large jug of water which he placed just out of my reach.

"Sit down," he commanded. A woman, the brunette from the club, appeared behind him holding a gun. I complied. The old boy came down to me, removed my gag and then untied my hands. He stank of BO. The creases in his face looked positively geological.

"What's this about, granddad?" I asked as he did the same for Johnny, who still looked out for the count.

"Dinner," he grunted.

"No, why are you doing this to us?"

"Justice, Mr Tyler," said the woman. "Justice."

"No justice, just us," mumbled the bloke, as she turned and left. Even at this low point in my rollercoaster life, I found myself thinking that she had great legs. A woman this fucked-up had no business looking so hot; she had a butt that would make Pippa swoon.

"I need a slash," exclaimed Johnny, in a voice loaded with anger and menace.

"Bucket's there."

"What if I need a crap?"

"As I said, the bucket's there."

John stood up defiantly, unzipped his flies and started pissing at the old man's boots.

He shrugged. "You animals have got to live with the stink," he said; and then he turned and walked back up the steps.

"I'll break your fucking neck, you old shit-cunt," John hollered.

Moments later the man returned and threw two bog rolls at us. Fucking Izal! I hated that at school. Just when you thought life couldn't get any worse. Still at least he left the light on.

Johnny tugged at the chain but it remained stubbornly attached to the brick wall.

"Well," I said glumly. "Looks like we've found our serial killer."

"Killers," he said equally morosely. "Just think I've got from a nice cosy berth at Her Majesty's pleasure, to this hole. How did they get you, H?"

"I tailed you to the NCP."

"What was you after, sloppy seconds?"

"Ha. Something like that."

"I wasn't expecting anything other than a bunk-up, she seemed so sweet and bright...and up for it."

"I had her at gun-point, then crack!"

"Enter the old bastard, stage right."

"Karma, John."

"Karma my arse. What is it with you filth? All Old Bill believe in fate. It's a myth, mate, another handy lie. You make your own luck in life, and that's the truth."

"D'you think?"

"I know."

"Well we'd better start making some of our own before these two clowns snuff it out for us."

"He's fucking mad – not in the sense of being angry, but as in carpet-chewing barking, bonkers, whacko, loony-tunes, doolally-tap."

John mimed playing a banjo, singing the opening notes of the music from Deliverance."Think they're related?" he asked.

"She's too good-looking, surely? I'll try and a look at her lug-holes next time. He's got ears like a fruit-bat."

Baker laughed. "That's it, the Man wanted to rub me out so they sent for fuckin' Batman...Batman and Throbbin', at least she'll get my throbbin' cock up her arse before I cut a throat."

"Attaboy Johnny, think positive."

"And as for soppy bollocks, that retarded fuckin' fuck-weasel..."

"How do you do it, JT?"

"Do what?"

"Swear like Gordon Ramsay without getting any of those ugly furrows in your forehead?"

"Just natural charm, I guess."

63

Westminster, London. Seven hours later

It had been Ken's idea to hire Church House Conference Centre for the rally. In an upmarket variation on his usual meeting room con, McManus had persuaded a sympathetic hereditary peer to book the centre under the name of 'Hope & Progress Solutions', although quite what the church janitor made of the motley crew who had turned up was anybody's guess. There were activists and representatives from all over Britain, a strange mix of types and ages. Tattooed young men and women straight from the terraces didn't exactly blend in with older fellows who looked like they'd be happier in a Masonic hall, and middle-aged ladies dressed for a church fete. Among their ranks were people from every shade of what the media would call far-Right opinion, ranging from the EDL to Ulster Loyalists, but also trade unionists and councillors, libertarians and populists, animal activists, active hooligans, ex-punks, ex-skinheads, police agents, spies, invited reporters and the odd vicar. Mostly they were white, with a few black and Asian faces, including a party of Sikhs. The security men looked they'd feel more at home on an ID parade or in a 1920s chain gang. A close look at their tattoos would have shown that there was nothing English about the ideology they actually followed.

The audience represented different types of simmering resentment – the disillusioned, the disgruntled, the angry and the betrayed, all drawn to this promise of a new dawn – the birth of a British Tea Party.

The venue capacity was 664, but as the *Guardian* would later work out, the two hard-working cameramen made that a handy 666 – all the better to demonise the faithful.

The star speaker, William Broadwick, had arrived half an hour ago in a series seven BMW supplied by a sympathetic VIP chauffeur hire boss. It had helped cheer him up after a hectic couple of hours composing a special column for the Sunday edition disassociating himself from the lunatic vigilante. He still felt shaken by the revelations, they had left him mortified.

William had been given a room, well stocked with fruit, bottled water and flowers. A stunning young woman who introduced herself as Charlotte knocked politely and told him she would be his PA for the evening. She looked a little French. He found her charming and she seemed in awe of him. Feeling flirtatious, William asked how she kept her figure so trim.

"I'm on the Mediterranean diet," she said with a smile that lit up the room.

Broadwick nodded. He had no time for fashionable food fads. His idea of a Mediterranean diet was smoking Gauloises between mugs of Ouzo in a holiday beach bar, but he smiled and said "Excellent. Lovely to meet you, my dear. Are you one of the event organisers?"

"No I'm just the hired help, but my father is a local activist. He's a big admirer of your columns Mr Broadwick – all of us are. We feel that you could turn us from a loose alliance of pressure groups into a mass movement that politicians would fear as well as hate. Together, we can make a difference."

"Yes, good, good," Broadwick responded, mentally calculating the positives and negatives of openly aligning himself with these people. Played right, it could net him a fortune. "As long as it stays within the law...," he added, thinking aloud.

"Oh yes. It's no use being radical if you can't present your ideas sensibly."

"Don't scare the horses. Do you know the running order for this evening?"

Charlotte produced a printed sheet. "You're the keynote speaker, Mr Broadwick. You're on at 8.30pm, after the warm-up speeches from our Southern co-ordinator Mike Phillips, and the Northern co-ordinator Ken McManus. After that, we'll take you straight to a smaller room for a press conference."

"And, umm, do I get paid after that?"

"Yes, immediately. I'll come looking for you, and take you to the treasurer. Will cash be okay?"

More than okay. Ideal, he thought.

"Cash is fine."

"Ha ha. Good. No paperwork, no VAT, and no nosy bureaucrat needs to know a thing about it. Happy days."

He smiled, she was delightful. "Indeed."

"And if you have time, we're laying on a little WS party for a select few afterwards."

Broadwick looked puzzled. WS? What the hell was that? Whores and swingers? WAGs and shags? Wank and spank?

"Wine and sandwiches," the exotic creature added, sensing his confusion. "Now we start in half an hour. Can I get you anything? Tea, coffee, a sandwich?"

"Whisky if you can find one."

"Of course. No problem Mr Broadwick."

He sank into a chair and re-read his speech. He had asked the news desk for guidance on Hope & Progress as soon as his agent had received the £5,000 offer for tonight's appearance. To his relief, the chief political reporter had assured him that they were not connected with the British National Party, that blundering creature of darkness led by fools and neo-fascists. Rather, they were a loose alliance of people disenchanted by the traditional parties' political myopia when it came to the everyday concerns of voters – the millions who dwelt in the vast hinterland beyond Westminster and Islington. His people.

***

The audience proved to be rowdy but good-natured. They clapped politely when Mike Phillips had turned his fire on UKIP, who he accused accurately of being "Thatcherite", and less accurately "a one-man band". He praised the party for keeping the European Union in the news but mocked its "extreme anti-racism policies" and "naive belief in the free market and the City of London". Instead, he advocated protectionism, import tariffs and bank nationalisation, which received a mixed response. Ken's speech went down much better, being a mix of solid jokes and tub-thumping populism; then William Broadwick was introduced. The columnist got a standing ovation before he'd even uttered a word.

Broadwick's speech was a clever one. It worked on two levels, playing to the audience here and the imagined one at Tory Central Office, whom he rightly suspected would be studying every word of it. Steering clear of anything that could be construed as extreme, William spoke about his "deep and undying love of Britain and England", identifying the EU, Hampstead liberals and self-hating race relations bores as the reasons for "this island's loss of culture, control, sovereignty and identity...the things our parents took for granted, the things they fought and died for, free speech, democracy, tolerance and decency NO LONGER EXIST."

There were cries of "Shame!", "No!" and a plaintive "Why?"

Broadwick warmed to his theme. He was British, he said, but he was English too and was "sickened to the pit of my stomach about being told that this was something to be ashamed of..."Then he threw in a decent joke, which he'd freshly purloined from *Private Eye*, about a secret government planning commission working on a redesign of the Union Jack. "They decided that they had to lose the red cross of St George, because its links to the Crusades made it offensive to non-Christians; they then decided to lose the red cross of St Patrick, as it was also a Christian reference not to mention a provocative reminder of Britain's imperialist oppression. They were then left with the blue saltire of St Andrew which obviously couldn't be kept on its own because it would be identical to the Scottish flag. So the great liberals thought hard and decided that the only workable solution would be get shot of all three crosses, leaving them with a new look Union Jack – a flag that was completely white and therefore entirely suitable for waving during future EU negotiations..."

Broadwick beamed as laughter engulfed the hall, and then he grew serious again for his big finish."Yes it's a joke, but how far is it from the truth? The political class has betrayed us again and again. They are quislings, traitors, sell-outs and shameless, bare-faced liars." The crowd cheered, Broadwick continued: "They tell us that the English people should be ashamed of our past. The opposite is true. The English have produced the greatest culture the world had ever seen...English genius still reverberates around the world. Not just Shakespeare, but Chaucer, Tallis, Purcell, Elgar, Kipling, Dickens, Browning and the rest. So when some jumped up Commie councillor tells you not to fly the English flag on St George's Day in case it 'offends' some hyper-sensitive follower of a hostile foreign medieval religion, laugh in their face and kick them straight out of office.

"You have the power, you, the English people, the Scots, the Welsh, the people of Northern Ireland, all of us British people – together, united, standing as one...we can make a difference, we must make a difference and by God we will shall make a difference, or else we will die trying."

The crowd were on their feet. They loved him, and they showed their love by cascading coins and notes into Ken's collecting buckets. His Hope and Progress movement was truly born.

Correction. Make that still-born. The press pack who were led to a smaller room for a question and answer session with the speakers were certainly smiling, but they were the smiles of a hungry crocodile waiting to strike. They pounced on Broadwick immediately, grilling him about the leaked links between his columns and the vigilante. On his back foot, William could do nothing except recycle quotes from tomorrow's big article, condemning the killer's unlawful actions unreservedly. A dark cloud embraced the pretty face of Charlotte, his temporary PA.

Just when he thought the worst of it was over, a man from the *Mail On Sunday* who resembled Aleksandr the advertising meerkat, stood up asked if he had anything to say on the subject of Jackie Sutton. Talk about dog eat dog! With a furious cry of "No comment!" Broadwick leapt to his feet and stomped out of the room with Charlotte a few feet behind him, her brow more furrowed than her father's fields.

"Are you okay, Mr Broadwick?"

"Yes. Yes," he said, recovering his composure. "It's just newspaper shenanigans."

"Jackie Sutton?"

"A private matter. Just a friend, a contact really. Gossip and slurs."

She led him back to his room where a thick set man with protruding ears – presumably his driver – was waiting.

"Did you mean what you said about the vigilante?"

"Oh yes, absolutely. I can't endorse that sort of terrorism. He's just as bad as the people he hunts down."

Charlotte held out her hand and stroked his cheek almost tenderly. "I'm so sorry you think like that," she said softly.

It was the last part of the night he would ever remember.

64

The Sunday papers had a field day. The Met authorised the release of Harry Tyler's true identity, and a cover story explaining away earlier reports of his death and his long absence as a major undercover operation into an international crime network which apparently stretched from Greater Manchester to the Urals.

The tale of the ex-con and the hero cop both kidnapped by a fringe terrorist group caught the imagination of editors and headline writers, and squeezed the story of William Broadwick's affair into second place, except in the *Mail On Sunday* which ran both news items as a split splash and the Express Group titles which ignored the sex scandal altogether. Both the *Sunday Express* and the *Daily Star Sunday* however were happy to run a prominent piece by their leading columnist condemning the vigilante "unreservedly". In a democratic society, he wrote, 'There can never be any excuse for taking the law into your own hands.'

Jackie Sutton's plan had worked perfectly. The *Mail*'s piece was unforgiving. It ran for five pages and included eight of Bang Bang Kirpachi's pictures of them kissing and canoodling, all of his quotes about their sex life, faithfully recorded by Paul Leather, a glamorous studio shot of her that the paper just happened to have found, and an unflattering one of Fiona getting a stiff cuddle from her husband. Both were quoted refusing to comment, but the *Mail* did helpfully reproduce ten fairly recent Broadwick column extracts on the related subjects of morality, fidelity and probity, under a shot of William looking particularly overweight along with the stinging caption: 'Broader-wick: putting the hippo in hypocrite.' Ouch.

Jackie was still chuckling about that as she enjoyed a luxurious full body massage in the spa she had booked for today. No one knew she was here; no one could contact her as she'd left her phone at home. She smiled as she relished the repercussions of the domestic train wreck she had set in motion, and looked forward to a full day of very expensive expert pampering. Tomorrow she'd meet Willie, tomorrow she'd tell him what she should have told him from day one: "It's my way, or the highway."

65

Tonbridge, Kent

"John. John!" I shook my sleeping cellmate, but he was still dead to the world. I had slept very deeply, far more deeply than anyone should on a wooden floor covered with hay. We must have been doped – they must have slipped something in the stew they gave us around midnight last night. What time was it? My watch was missing, I strained my eyes in the gloom. His was luminous; it said 11.57am.Something was different. What? Not the smell, the room still stank. Then I heard a murmur from the other side of John. It was someone else. They brought us a new play mate.

"Hello," I said loudly. "Who's there?" I shook John again. "Come on JB, we've got company."

66

The decision to plant a bomb at the offices of Suszem, Tillett & Hertz had been an easy one to make. They were the solicitors who had represented the Tonbridge travellers in their battle against the local council. It had been planted last night, with some degree of poetic justice, with William Broadwick unconscious in the back of the Ford Transit. It was Broadwick who had condemned the firm as 'rapacious parasites bloated on legal aid, defending the undefendable'.

The bomb exploded late on Sunday morning, long after the comatose columnist had been deposited in the Stevens' cellar. The farm stock had expanded to include one villain, one apparently heroic undercover police officer and their very own gutless Judas.

Broadwick had proved to be as weak and worthless as the politicians whom he routinely denounced, and yet their new captive was an unexpected bonus, an instrument to be used for the benefit of the cause.

67

Tonbridge, Kent. 11.50am

Bat Ears and the brunette turned up as before; him carrying sandwiches and water, her carrying a shotgun. Keeping his distance from John, he circled round to the third man and removed his gag.

Not smart. The posh prick launched into a "Don't you know who I am?" tirade, punctuated with fucks and threats. "What's all this about, Charlotte?" he demanded.

"Of course we know who you are," said the woman. "You're the man who let us all down. How many pieces of silver did it take to buy your soul, Mr Broadwick?"

Ah, so this was Fleet Street's finest, he looked a lot older than his newspaper by-line picture, a lot fatter too.

"I don't know who the Devil you think you are..." the newcomer grumbled.

"Oi! Shut the fuck up!" barked John.

William Broadwick bit his lip.

Bat Ears took the gun, and the brunette called Charlotte began to film us on her Blackberry.

"This had better be for HBO, darlin'," leered Johnny. "Here, get my good side."

Charlotte ignored him.

"She's cocking a deaf'un, John," I said.

"She's playing hard to get, that's all. But you have to know darling I like to be in charge. There's only one time I can suffer being under a woman."

"You've got a foul mind," snarled the old man.
"Just being friendly, pops. You don't mind, do ya darling? It turns you on, don't it?"

Charlotte finished filming but still ignored him. I tried appealing to their better nature. "Listen both of you, you've already broken more laws than I can count. Why not stop this nonsense now? Let us go, and I'll testify that you cooperated. I've got a great defence brief, who will take your case all the way to Strasbourg..."

Big mistake. The old man flared up. "I would rather die than be judged by those jumped-up jackasses in Europe," he seethed. "You're a police officer, you know how much damage these foreign courts do. You should be on our side! We are doing your job for you. We're raining fire and brimstone down on those the Law should punish but won't."

He had a point. "But with respect," I said. "Who are you to take the place of the courts? I'm no fan of the EU, and the law needs reform, of that I'm in no doubt, but you can't put yourself above it. You have made yourself judge, jury and executioner. Who gave you that authority?"

"The only ones who can, Mr Tyler," answered the brunette. "The people, and God Almighty."

"How did the people authorise what you're doing?" I asked, choosing to swerve the God squad guff.

"It's happening today," she replied. "In a very modern way. And tomorrow, God willing, we will see justice acted out. Mr Broadwick here will be our instrument, if he knows what's good for him."

"It will be his chance to redeem himself in the eyes of the followers he has let down," the old man added.

"But that makes you as bad as Baker," I said, trying to find an angle that could penetrate his mental shield of certainty. "You're a murderer too."

"No. Because I have a code. Without a code a man is just a thug, a murderer, a sociopath. I have the code!"

The brunette weighed in with "If you can't beat the bad guys within the law, you have to beat them without it."

The old man's eyes glazed over. "Once war has been forced on society, then good men have no alternative but to end it as quickly as possible. The object of war is to win it, not to drag it out as long as possible. Endless violence is the product of indecision. No one wants that. When you're in a war, as we are today, what you're fighting for, the one thing you are fighting for, is victory. If you go for appeasement, like we did with Saddam in the 90s, we're just postponing the inevitable, and postponing makes thing worse. Bloodier. More damaging."

"The liberals, the weak, the pacifists, give the enemy advantage after advantage," said the brunette. "He knows that," she pointed at Broadwick, adding bitterly. "At least, he did until yesterday."

"I come from a line of old soldiers," said Bat Ears. "And we either die or fade away. I don't mind dying, but fading away isn't for me."

"I understand, and believe me as a cop I sympathise. But how can you be so certain about what's right and wrong? What is this code you talk about?"

"I told you," he snapped. "The good book. The Ten Commandments. Thus saith the Lord: 'Keep justice and do righteousness for my salvation is about to come and my righteousness to be revealed...'"

Ho boy!

"I saw the light," said John in a soft rasp, his eyes blazing with conviction. "In prison, about eighteen months in. I realised the errors of my way. I repented. I let the Lord into my life and was born again..."

He sounded so sincere he almost had me believing him. The woman called Charlotte smiled. "Nice try, Baker. Unfortunately for you, I met you at a party remember? A party where you drank alcohol, offered me cocaine and was prepared to leave your girlfriend on the dance floor while you came and had sex with me in the back of a car. Your soul is more lost than the British Empire. A man like you can no more be reformed than a feral dog."

"Okay, you've got me. So here's another idea, come back here and drain me spuds.Old Batman can film that for you. That'll get you viewers. It might even spur you on it. Who was it said that sexual excess is the engine for violence?"

"Gandhi," she replied coldly. "You know I was thinking, before we do the execution, maybe we should give the public a taste of the righteous joy to come. You're a very virile, sexy man Johnny, so perhaps a free, freelance penile amputation would appeal. With anaesthetic of course, we're not animals."

He shot her a glare she could have shaved her legs with. "That will never ever happen."

"We'll see. I can't think of a more wretched end for a big strutting macho man than losing his manhood on YouTube before his life devoted to the service of Satan is snuffed out in the name of the Lord."

Satan? FFS!"Once you see it, you'll want it," John replied, as cocky as you like.

She scowled at him. "And after that, castration Mr Baker. Complete emasculation. It's only right and fitting, after all we all know that the Devil is smooth between the legs."

For once, even Johnny Too kept quiet. Charlotte turned and followed her father upstairs.

"I bet your dick just got a whole lot shorter, John."

"Thanks for that, arsehole."

William Broadwick was shaking. "What did she mean, I'll be her instrument?" he asked.

"Fuck knows, I'll be her fucking instrument for sure though after I've topped that bat-eared fuck. Fuckin' Satan? I'll make sure she has the Devil in her before all this is over – smoothly, between her legs. Or roughly. I'm not fussed."

"But she said I'd..."

"Shut it, prick. It ain't all about you."

"Except that you've been their inspiration from the start, Mr Broadwick," I said calmly. "You've been thundering away in your column, giving it large as the likes of us would say, and they've been acting on it. What has happened to make them change their mind about you?"

"I umm, I denounced them, or at least him, at a public meeting last night. The girl was posing as a backstage assistant. She took me back to my room afterwards and the next thing I can remember is coming round in this hell-hole."

"Ah, I get it. You disowned the old boy's vigilante crusade. He thought he was doing what you wanted him to do, and in his eyes you stabbed him in the back."

"I have never condoned violence."

"Maybe not, but I seem to remember you making excuses for the man or men who killed a paedophile and a porn baron, which to him would have read like an endorsement. There is no way he and that weird bird are going to let you get off the ride now. What was it Chandler wrote? Ah yeah, 'There's no trap so deadly as the trap you set yourself'..."

I looked at the blubbery writer and tried hard not to stare at the rapidly spreading wet patch on his hand-tailored Prince Of Wales check suit trousers.

"John," I said. "No disrespect, but to them you are the enemy, I'm a good guy and Broadwick here is an idol with feet of clay; so next time they come down here, let me and Billy boy do the talking. If we stay calm, and speak their language, we might just be able to talk them out of whatever they have got in mind."

"Nice theory Harry, but the talking ship has sailed, alongside any ships you might be thinking of marked peaceful resolution or sanity. These people are beyond nuts. They've killed, they've bombed and they've kidnapped. We're talking bats in the belfry. Their oars ain't touching the water, bruv. They'll no more listen to you than these brick walls will. This is down to us, bruv, you and me. We've got to figure out a way to get out of here. Otherwise we're all brown bread."

William Broadwick made a strange whining high-pitched noise, like a bagpiper drowning slowly in mucus, and passed out. I ignored him.

"Okay, we know they're both crazy, but they're also straight. They're clever, not cunning. They have a set of rules that they stick to, whereas we know how to break and bend them."

"It's what I've done all of me life."

"That's the difference John, we're crafty as well as smart, and when we get the chance we will be absolutely merciless. The Marquis of Queensberry is out the door."

68

Royal Tunbridge Wells, midday.

Gary Shaw got to the Toad Rock Retreat as soon as it opened and was relieved to see Thelma behind the jump. She seemed to have a warm glow about her today. The detective ordered a pint of light and bitter and offered her "one for yourself", which she accepted "for later" as was her custom.

"Have you seen Mick lately, Thelma? Do you know where he is now?"

"You must be psychic, officer, he's upstairs fixing the electrics. I'll give him a shout."

She buzzed the intercom and said, "Michael, there's someone to see you, it's dinner time anyway so you might as well take a break. We don't want to tire you out..."

An unusually cheerful Mick Neale materialised in moments. He was unshaven and wearing an orange T-shirt with a slogan that read 'Praia de Burgau beach bum'.

"I take it that's Portugal," said Gary Shaw, shaking his hand. "Pint?"

"I'll have a Guinness with you, Gal. Great sardines, amazing cataplanas..."

"I'll check it out; I'll need somewhere to live when I take early retirement, which frankly can't come soon enough. Guinness here please, Thelma."

"Will you be wanting dinner too, Mr Shaw?" she asked. "Roast beef, chicken or lamb today with all the trimmings."

"Lamb will do a treat, thanks. Can I run a tab?"

"I'm not so sure," she smiled. "You look a shady character to me."

"Definitely a wrong'un," agreed Mick. "All these Londoners coming down here with their funny ways..."

They moved to a small table.

"So have you got anywhere with the vigilante, Gary?"

"I'm off it, Mick. You know it escalated?"

"I saw the papers. A double kidnapping now..."

"And a bomb that went off a couple of hours ago, blew the front windows off a solicitor's in town. Almost certainly the same deal as the one at Europe House. Home-made, rudimentary timer. At least no casualties this time."

"So you're off the case completely?"

"Yeah, big boys' rules now. You sure you've got no idea who could be behind this? We're pretty sure it's someone local."

"No. Well. Maybe. I dunno. I was pretty certain that it couldn't be old man Stevens because he's so gaga these days. But Len the landlord at this place bumped into him in the week and said he was absolutely the full shilling, alert, coherent, and almost perky. Then I ran into Charlie on Thursday and she was quite off with me, told me not to come round for a while, said they didn't have the money to pay me..."

"Which is possible because everyone's business is up shit creek at the moment and the banks are busy confiscating all the paddles..."

"True, but hear me out, Gary. One other thing, I heard a report on that first bomb, how it was made. The last time I was at the Stevens farm, I saw a load of chemicals in one of the barns, ones I'd never seen there before."

"Which again could be a coincidence, but..."

"But put that all together and that's enough to set off the old mental alarm bells."

"So it could be worth giving the Stevens place a spin..."

"How quickly can you get a search warrant?"

69

Woking, Surrey

Fiona Broadwick had been annoyed when her husband had not returned home last night, wrongly assuming William had spent the night with his tart. And when her home phone started ringing off the hook, she chose to ignore it, suspecting it was Willie hoping to placate her with a fresh load of lies, apologies and assurances. She didn't get around to bringing the Sunday papers in from the porch until half past ten and was alarmed to see a pack of press at her fence, along with photographers who started clicking the moment she opened her front door.

Fiona sat down to absorb the headlines. Willie kidnapped? Held hostage? She thought for a moment and then did what any well-connected wronged wife would do in such a dreadful situation. She found her husband's contact book and rang Max Clifford at home. She'd met the publicist at a charity event near his Surrey home when William had been booked as auctioneer – a last minute replacement for Jeffrey Archer. Their telephone conversation was brief but extremely profitable. He told her to stay in the house, and not to answer the phone. Her exclusive story – he called it a buy-up – was probably worth £40,000 to the right newspaper, more if they negotiated a tie-in piece in *Hello* or *OK!*, and much more if she held some sensational revelations for the ghost-written autobiography he could also arrange. True to his word, Max had done the deal in under an hour.

At 1.30pm, she was taken from the house with a coat over her head and sped away to a hotel in Surbiton in a 4x4 with blackened windows.

70

Royal Tunbridge Wells, Kent

Gary Shaw and Mick Neale finished their dinners, Mick sank the dregs of his second pint of Guinness, Shaw had switched to tea. He had a decision to make, go to his guv'nor or take a chance and go for a 'freelance' sniff about. At around 2.15pm, the breaking news on TV forced his hand. Headlined 'New Vigilante Video', Sky News cut to YouTube footage of the three hostages in their dingy basement cell while the traditional 'voice of an actor' recited the words of a press statement dictated to the PA. The message was straightforward and uncompromising. The public was invited to vote for and against the televised execution of the former South London gangster Johnny Baker, the task to be carried out by no less a media favourite than William Broadwick. To vote 'Yes' to kill, viewers had merely to 'like' the short YouTube clip. To save Baker, they should just 'unlike' it. Any attempt to remove the video from the site would be interpreted as a Yes vote.

The method of execution was left unstated, but Gulliver Stevens had already decided that the gangster would be killed by being repeatedly Tasered through the skull. His electrified corpse would then be chopped up, put through the meat grinder and fed to the pigs – by which he meant turned into hamburgers and sold from a van outside Tonbridge cop shop. All except for his head. The farmer had considered sticking it on a pole like they used to do, but had decided that sewing it onto the corpse of an ass and depositing it outside the Old Bailey would be far more memorable, not to mention sweet poetic justice.

71

Tonbridge, Kent

William Broadwick was dribbling, a revolting sight but marginally preferable to seeing and hearing weep and whine. John took great pleasure in winding him up and had embarked on a lengthy discussion with him on the contradictions between claiming to be a libertarian while opposing the decriminalisation of narcotics.

Broadwick went into a rant about drug culture which had started around jazz and "degenerate rock 'n' roll sub-music" and had been fanned by Hollywood and "the evil of television."

Johnny laughed. "You're supposed to be a Tory, pal, you're supposed to believe in free markets, but you're as much of a control freak as the fuckin' Reds. Now I happen to like some of the high classical music you like, but you like it not just because of its power and sweep but because you're a snob and it makes you feel superior to me and 'im who drop our Hs..."

"And break the law!" he snapped back. "Yes, what's wrong with feeling superior to common criminals?"

"Two points. One, I'm happy to break any law made up by pricks like you, and two, as you shouldn't need reminding we are actually being held here by your fan club, a pair of fucked-up psycho-killers whose vigilante fantasies have been brought to the boil by years of reading your self-righteous bollocks, my son."

If William Broadwick had a clever reply to that, he kept it to himself. Instead the famously splenetic columnist just said sorry.

"Sorry?" sneered Johnny. "That's tits on a bull, pal. Useless."

The fucked-up psycho-killers turned up moments later, as if on cue, and they brought us the same poxy stew as they had done the night before. The old man seemed a little greyer than before, though.

"I won 6 shillings and 4d yesterday," he told me.

"Really? That's nice for you, grandad."

"6 shillings and 4d, playing three card brag."

"Come on Dad," snapped the brunette, leading him away by the arm.

"Stay frosty, darlin'," Johnny shouted.

"Don't eat the stew," I muttered under my breath to John, as they locked the cellar door behind them. "The more I think about it, the more I'm sure they're drugging it, and we need to keep our wits about us."

"Fuck, okay. But I'm so hungry I'd eat the balls off a low-flying duck."

We never said anything to Broadwick, who despite his heightened emotional state managed to polish off two bowls of the stuff.

"You want to eat some Alpen, son," Johnny sneered. "Get yerself some more nuts."

Broadwick pulled a face and sulked. But not for long. He had passed out within about ten minutes.

"Thank fuck for that," I said. "No more bleating and belly-aching."

"If you hear them coming again, make out you're out cold too."

"It was fuckin' cold last night. As cold as an Eskimo's ice-hole in here."

"I haven't been so cold since the lodger stole the duvet. All you could hear was the sound of brass monkeys weeping and of soppy bollocks moaning and groaning in his sleep."

"He wouldn't be much use in your game, John. Imagine him under interrogation, he'd spill like the Exxon Valdez."

"He's like the class grass. Every time that pair of pricks come down here I expect him to put his hand up and say, 'Please sir, I heard Baker threatening to "bash the granny out of an old cunt" and I think he means you'."

"What do you make of Bat Ears?"

"Bats in the belfry too, seems like dementia to me."

"Yeah. He's losing it."

"A short-arse little fucker, ain't he?"

"Yeah, we're definitely talking Napoleon syndrome, short man compensating."

"Let's hope he's prepared to meet his Johnny Too Waterloo."

"What about the girl?"

"Well, you've spoken to her."

"In Stringfellows, pissed, when she had me iron like a lion in Zion."

"But smart?"

"Very. She's a bright one, very sharp."

"And quite capable of violence."

"I don't doubt it. But he's the one, in'e? He's the nut-job, the fruit loop. The daughter is obviously just going along with what he wants to keep the old man happy. Got to be...If we had time to separate them, talk to her rationally."

"Yeah, big if though mate. I don't think we do."

Johnny glanced over at Broadwick. "Funny thing is, he's got a lot of fans inside. The old cons, they're suckers for all that hang 'em, flog 'em stuff."

"He fights a bloody good fight, behind a keyboard."

"Don't they all?"

"So what now? You got a plan?"

"Not much of one," Johnny Too said, taking one of the spoons and squirreling it away in his suit pocket. "But it's better than none at all."

72

Gary Shaw asked Neale to take him down to the Stevens farm. They observed the place through Mick's bird-watching binoculars for about an hour and a half in the drizzling rain, but there was no sign of any activity other than the old man watching TV. Certainly nothing suspicious, and the rumbling, grumbling skies above threatened worse weather ahead.

"Maybe come back in the morning," suggested Mick. "We can think of a reason why I'd turn up unannounced. Maybe the boiler, they had problems with it last Winter. You could be a plumber."

Shaw nodded. He liked Mick Neale. He was solid, as hard as cave-aged cheddar and reliable with it; a good man to have around.

"Okay, good idea. If we can get through the door it'd put my mind at rest. I've got to go into the office first though. I'll call you."

73

Monday's newspapers found a dozen different ways to headline the impending horror –Day Of Judgement, Hours From Death, YouTube Euthanasia – but the *Sun* said it most starkly and succinctly; its splash screamed Execution Day. Most reported that the public vote was overwhelmingly in favour of the DIY death penalty, although the *Guardian* report went bigger on Twitter, where #butcherBaker had trended early but was rapidly overtaken by a #SaveJT campaign.

The *Mail* ran a piece by Richard Littlejohn, a long-time opponent of capital punishment, calling for restraint; the *Daily Star* with cheery insouciance, ran a spread helpfully featuring their artist's impressions of the different ways the execution could be carried out: rope, axe to the head, gassing, poison, acid bath, barbiturate overdose, home-made guillotine or shotgun. An online bookmaker ran with it and was offering odds on how it would happen.

Sky News, meanwhile, had rounded up friends and relatives of the hostages, including an *Express* colleague of Broadwick's who testified to the columnist's resolute nature and "courage under fire". Kay Burley also interviewed a dietician claiming to be an ex-fiancé of Harry Tyler, ex-cop Rachel Freeman-Hartley (née Freeman, formerly Rachel Morley, remarried 2012, currently separated) who described him as "the love of my life" in a voice with a strong Salford twang. They'd had a one night stand in 1986! Still it was a nice plug for her latest diet book, *Mind Over Platter – Think Yourself Thin*.

In South London, Johnny Baker's angry friends and family had been assembled by Slobberin' Ron. Tempers were running high. The word had gone out across the manor and beyond – from Kidbrooke to Camberwell, Bermondsey to Tulse Hill, Rotherhithe to Lee: 'John's in trouble'. Old faces, young faces, bits of kids who only knew of the Bakers as an underworld legend; all of them were on standby.

There wasn't much they could do yet, but they were tooled up, they were scanning internet coverage and watching Sky News, ready and waiting.

74

Tonbridge, Kent; 9am

Rhona Watts had been doing the *Telegraph* crossword as she waited for Gary Shaw to arrive at the station. She had news. Essex CID had finally sent through CCTV footage of Simon Loewry on the day of his murder. It showed him leaving a pub and a wine bar with an attractive dark-haired woman. Shaw got straight on the phone to Mick Neale, who arrived fifteen minutes later in a Peter Tosh T-shirt and a flying jacket.

"Is it Glastonbury time already?" laughed Wattsie.

"Very funny Rhona. You should be on the stage."

"Mick, we think we've got the killer," Gary Shaw said urgently. "And I think I know who she is, but I need you to I.D. her. Do you know this woman?"

Wattsie hit play on the DVD in her PC. Mick peered at the screen, wishing he'd brought his bins, hoping the image was clear enough for him to see her face. It was.

"It's her, Gary. That is our Charlie."

"Are you certain?"

"100 per cent."

"Loewry mentioned he was seeing a Lotte to an employee."

"Exactly. Charlie is a Charlotte. Charlie, Lotte...they're both..."

"Derivations of the same name...so her and the old man are working together as a team."

"Certainly looks that way."

Gary Shaw paused and thought about his options. It didn't take long. "Right, Mick can you come with me back to the farm? Odds on that's where they've got their hostages."

"In the cellar, I'd have thought Gary. She had me clear it out a while back. Not conclusive, but it has brick walls just like the place where the YouTube scene was shot."

"And it's our best shot. Rhona, get on to everyone – S015, the Armed Response Unit, the Chief Super, anyone who can get there quickly. But tell them I've gone on ahead because that execution is planned for about half an hour's time. What's the address, Mick?"

Mick Neale wrote it down for her.

"I'll tell the boss, guv, make the calls and see you there."

"Wear body armour."

"What about you?"

Shaw was half-way out the door already. "No time," he shouted back.

Rhoda Watts glanced down at the near completed crossword on her desk. The final clue was 'Keep tabs on spouse'. The solution, she knew, was Checkmate. She hoped to hell it was a sign.

75

Charlotte Stevens had been an only child, ferociously intelligent and cute enough to wrap every male she ever met around her little finger. The death of her mother at ten years old had traumatised both her and her father. Her time in state education system ended soon after. Charlotte's Dad hated the comprehensive school system which had "signalled the death of excellence", and as he couldn't afford to send her private, the girl was home schooled by a retired English teacher Gulliver knew from their local church. She taught the child maths, English, history and science; he passed on his political and social views along with an interpretation of Christianity which was heavy on Old Testament values.

A talented but self-sufficient girl, Charlotte seemed uninterested in making friends with children her own age. She only mixed with other kids at church and at her karate lessons. An outside observer might have thought her obsessive; almost certainly Charlotte was somewhere on the autism spectrum. By the age of seventeen she was a black belt, at eighteen she added four A levels to her haul of eleven GCSEs. She could have breezed into any University in the land, instead she signed up for an Agriculture and combined Farm Management BSc course.

Sexually, she had been a late developer, but her appetite for cock was ravenous. Her father would never have approved, so she developed her alter ego Lotte on dating sites and Facebook, meeting strangers for sex as often as possible. Married men were safest, and the most grateful.

Two years ago, when her father told her that God had spoken to him, she hadn't been fazed, in fact she believed him. The Almighty had told Gulliver Stevens that William Broadwick was His herald, His John the Baptist and that he should interpret his writings and act upon them, for the humble farmer was the new Messiah. And recently, as the cruel curse of ageing had nibbled away at his mind, leaving it too fogged up to do God's work, Charlotte was happy to step into the breach, using any means necessary, including debasing her own body, to rid the world of evil. Wearing her father's clothes, she had executed the child killer, planted bombs and rained fire and brimstone on the travellers. His work was important. It was a divine mission; it had to be finished.

***

Johnny Too had spent half the night working away at the screws that kept his chain attached to the wall with the end of the metal spoon. "It's like Colditz all over again," he'd muttered, before tunelessly whistling the Dambusters' March. When he finished, I did the same. It must have been dusk by the time I'd worked the last screw out. We then placed them loosely back into position. We didn't bother with Broadwick's chain; he had been comatose throughout, snoring like a buzz saw cutting through a steel pipe.

The plan, such as it was, was for me to distract our cranky captors and him to jump whoever had the gun.

"And if it doesn't work..." I'd started saying.

"Better to die on your feet that live on your knees, H. The crack of a whip is a sound I'll never get used to."

"I'm with you on that."

"I know you can't see it, but prison did change me, Harry. I used the time. I even started to appreciate things like Hinduism. They're right, life is a wheel of eternal frustration, struggle and – if we're lucky – upgrades through reincarnation."

"What would you be reincarnated as?"

He thought for a moment and replied: "A pigeon."

"Why, to shit on the bastards below?"

"No because pigeons fuck forty times a day – that's something else I learnt in there."

***

William Broadwick came around late morning, grumbling and grunting. To make matters worse, he needed a crap. We averted our eyes as he perched his fat arse over the bucket. The stench was dreadful, almost painful.

"Christ, what died up your arse?" asked John, who began to shout and holler to attract our captors' attention.

"I should nick the bastard for dumping toxic waste," I moaned. "Christ. This place needs ventilation."

"All three of these cunts need ventilation, with 9milimetre bullets. COME ON! GET DOWN 'ERE!"

Charlotte appeared first, with Bat Ears behind, clutching his shotgun and looking out of sorts. He had a face on him like a forgotten tennis ball that had been left greying for a year in the Wimbledon guttering.

"Can you get shot of this shit sharpish, please?" John asked. "Pretty please?"

She came down the stairs, taking care to stay out of John's reach. I distracted the old man by shouting "Sir! Behind you!" – yeah, that old one. Only there was actually something behind him, a small but aggressive-looking Burmese cat. As Bat Ears turned, John jack-knifed to his feet and ran at the woman, jerking his chain from the wall and taking her by surprise. The old fella swung round, whereupon the cat jumped on his head, digging his claws in. The shock made him discharge his weapon harmlessly into the ceiling. The blast added to the mounting confusion. I was deafened by it, I guess we all were. Broadwick jumped to his feet and accidentally stepped into the bucket of crap. The cat then jumped on his head, claws extended. Broadwick made a noise like a vegetarian drowning in a cauldron of meat madras, simultaneously scared, pained and disgusted, before sliding back down to the floor.

John slapped Charlotte to the ground and squared up to Bat Ears, who looked suddenly lost and vacant, shaking his head as if he had cerebral palsy. I took the opportunity to push past him and rush up the stairs to the door.

John took the shotgun from his hand and was about to chin him with the butt when Charlotte jumped up and crowned him with the shit bucket, leaving a trail of faeces across her father's lumberjack shirt. Baker was a big, muscular man and heavy set but she caught him easily enough – on top of her martial arts training, a decade of boxercise and yoga had left her with incredible upper body strength. She dragged the gangster back to where he'd started from.

"Dad," she snapped. "DAD! DAD!"

The old man came out of his trance.

"Tie him up again by his arms and feet and gag the bastard. He can stay like that until the main event."

She grabbed the gun and went looking for the escaped prisoner – me.

76

Outside the farm, Gary Shaw and Mick Neale heard the shot.

"That's it, come on, we're going in," Shaw said urgently. "Give me your baton and grab a tool of any kind."

Mick handed over his police issue cosh and picked up an axe handle, following the detective to the back door of the farmhouse. Shaw turned the handle and pushed it open, slowly and quietly. Inside, dogs were barking and a parrot was squawking. Above that racket, no one heard them come in. Shaw motioned for Neale to check the ground floor, while he edged his way up the stairs.

77

There had to be a weapon somewhere. Coming out of the cellar, I kicked open a couple of downstairs doors, then headed up to the bedrooms. People like this would be odds-on to keep some protection where they slept. I dived into the first room, rolled over the bed towards the side that was furthest from the door and dropped down into the narrow gap between the bed and the wall. The bottom of the bed was low but I managed to get my left arm under it, feeling around until I reached something hard and barrel-like.

"Come out now!" A woman's voice. Charlotte. I grabbed my tool and pulled it out triumphantly. It was a Rampant Rabbit. So I'm guessing this was her room then.

"Get up now, or I swear I'll shoot you clean through the bed."

I stood up, letting the vibrator clatter to the floor. Charlotte was pointing the gun straight at me. This was it then. Looks like my last few grains of luck had clean drained away. Karma? Karma'n'get-me.

Both of us heard the Armed Response Unit vehicles screech into the farmyard, and skid to a scrunching halt. I listened to the car doors slamming and tried to work out how many cops there were. At least eight I reckoned, the odds were getting better. Charlotte stood on the bed, trying to look over my shoulder and clock the scene below. Suddenly Gary Shaw came charging into the room with his baton drawn. He rugby tackled her, sending her flying. As Charlotte fell back, she dropped the shotgun but put her hands over her shoulders and pushed herself back upright with striking athletic grace. I went to grab her and was knocked flying by a powerful kick. Shaw caught her other leg and was rewarded with a heel kick to the kidney. As he rolled in agony she inserted two fingers into his nostrils and fish-hooked him off the bed. Fucking hell, that had to hurt. The gun was back in her hands.

Charlotte motioned for me to raise my hands. I complied. I didn't have much option.

"You can still get out of this," I said. "Give me the gun, Charlotte. Let your Dad take the rap."

"Shut up!" she snapped.

"He's not well, he won't go to jail. He needs psychiatric treatment, he's not right in the head."

She pointed the piece at me, her mouth a perfect curve of disgust. I felt vulnerable, dominated; and for a moment that in itself seemed unexpectedly exciting. No. Stay focused. From behind her Gary Shaw made another lunge, but she heard him. She spun round and fired. The round grazed the outside of his left thigh and as he fell back he hit his head on the wall and sparked right out. My ears hurt like buggery. It occurred to me that that was her last shot, but she'd realised it too and had leapt over his body to get the Beretta out of her bedside drawer. She was up on the bed again, the pistol aimed at my head...

78

The door to the cellar was wide open when Mick Neale passed. He looked down and was unsurprised to see Johnny Too bound and gagged.

A sudden noise behind him, made him spin around. It was Gulliver Stevens, holding a Luger.

"Michael my dear boy, how are you?"

"I'm fine Mr Stevens, I've erh, just popped round to sort out those things you asked me to take care of. I was going to start down in the cellar. Is that okay?"

"Of course. You get started, my boy. I'll make us a pot of tea."

Silly old doddery fool, thought Mick. He started down the stairs. He made the first two steps before the stock of the Luger connected with the back of his skull, sending him flying into a mess of human waste. He was out cold.

Gulliver Stevens shut the cellar door and locked it. Then he retired to his office and sat behind the desk, rocking to and fro and whistling softly.

79

Camera crews from Sky News and the BBC arrived at the scene about twenty minutes after the cops. That had been about an hour or so ago. We were the day's big story. BBC1 dropped its scheduled programming to show the action as it unfolded.

Charlotte seemed remarkably calm. She'd handcuffed me to her wardrobe with cuffs that looked a damn sight more Ann Summers than *Scott & Bailey*, and made contact with the senior officer, DCI Laurie Rouman.

Speaking slowly and clearly, she informed him that she had four hostages, including two police officers, one of whom was injured. In return for their safe release, she wanted a police helicopter to take her and her father to a destination of her choice, and as a goodwill gesture she was prepared to release the injured officer immediately.

Rouman said he'd get back to her. She told me to look out the window again. Crowds had started to gather along the lane – held back by a police cordon. Three quarters of an hour later, with clearance from the Home Office sought and obtained, her mobile rang. Charlie spoke briefly to Rouman, then hung up and beamed, "Game on."

She uncuffed me and made me carry Gary Shaw, who was now semi- conscious, down the stairs. I left him outside the back door, and watched through the glass as the paramedics came and collected him.

Charlie found her father in the office. He was in a bad way.

"I'm putting you back in the cellar Mr Tyler," she said. "There's nothing we can do now except wait for the helicopter."

At least that meant the execution was off. One way or another, we'd have closure today. But then again the pits had closures, it's not always a good thing.

***

Charlotte Stevens packed a travel bag, throwing in passports, cash, credit cards and a change of clothes. Everything had gone horribly pear-shaped, but at least she could still get her father away from the wreckage. She had friends in Normandy; they could hang out at their farm until she figured out what to do next. Back in her room, she switched on the TV for the Six O'Clock News. She was pleased with the coverage. The BBC report had highlighted many of their political demands, while Sky News was running them repeatedly across the bottom of the screen. If nothing else, the message was getting across.

When Sky cut to a profile of William Broadwick, she tutted and switched back to the Beeb.

Half an hour later, her phone rang again. DCI Rouman informed her that the chopper had landed in a field about half a mile from the house.

"So how are we going to do this then?"

"What would you suggest?"

"Okay, you'll need to drive us to the helicopter. Withdraw all your men from the yard and send in one vehicle. I shall let my father out first, then John Baker and the other police officer, Mr Tyler, who will both be free to leave the farm. Finally I shall come out with William Broadwick. I shall have him at gunpoint. We will both get in the car with my father and be driven to the helicopter, where I will give the pilot my instructions. If I am convinced that you are not trying to double-cross us, I shall then release Broadwick."

"We won't double-cross you."

"There may be fatalities if you do."

"That is understood."

"Good, my father will be out shortly."

She turned out her bedroom light and watched the armed police withdraw from the farm, then she went down to the office and collected the old man. She led him to the back yard, kissed his forehead and said "Wait for me in the car Dad, with the nice driver."

She took a deep breath, picked up the Beretta and unlocked the door to the cellar. She saw Harry Tyler and Johnny Baker at the bottom of the steps – Baker now untied, by Tyler she guessed, but that didn't matter. To his left sat the shit-stained gibbering wreck of William Broadwick.

"Okay, this is what is going to happen," she said as she walked down the stairs. "Mr Broadwick is going to stay sitting where he is and you two are going to follow m..."

She never got to finish the sentence. She couldn't. Mick Neale was standing over her fallen body, swinging his axe handle.

80

I left the farmhouse slowly, feeling like an old, punch-drunk prize-fighter who had just gone fifteen rounds with the new champ. The sky was off-colour, like an inverted unwashed soup tureen, and it was noisy. There was a whole crowd of people waiting for us to come out. A heavy-breasted woman in a floral Miu Miu shirt and Zara jodhpurs who turned out to be Broadwick's bit on the side, and Maxine Slater, Johnny's bit of posh, in a Prada light denim-look two-piece. Both were dressed wildly impractically for a farm siege, either because they'd left home in a hurry or more likely because they'd wanted to look good in tomorrow's papers...

I didn't see anyone waiting for me until I walked past the 4x4 and recognised Wattsie Watts, who waved, then I saw Knockers – what the fuck was she doing here? – and then Rosie, the little rockabilly barmaid from the 12 Bar, which was even more surprising. Ho boy! Complicated. How was I going to juggle this one?

There was a bigger shock to come though – because finally, behind a scrum of press photographers hollering my name, I saw something which actually made my heart stop. It was Kara, and she had the kids with her.

Now my heart was in my mouth. You might be thinking 'spoilt for choice' but there was only one way this could go. I dropped to my knees and held out my arms. The uniformed cops let the children run up and throw their arms around me. Their love was unqualified. I wasn't so sure about Kara's. Twenty different emotions flooded across that beautiful face, relief, joy, anger, sorrow, compassion, regret, love...I'd like to think, but you could never tell with her...all competing for dominance.

Her eyes were still striking – blue-green, like Cornish coral. I leaned forward and kissed her lightly on the cheek, savouring the familiarity of her scent. Just the smell of her shampoo triggered a tidal wave of suppressed memories. I wanted to hug her and kiss her properly but couldn't second guess how she'd react to that. Before I could say anything, I heard someone cough behind me.

"Harry?"

It was a posh but genial voice belonging to a tall, handsome middle-aged man with barely a trace of grey in his jet-black hair.

"Laurie Rouman," he said. "Excellent job. I need to get you all down the station as soon as possible, either to be debriefed or to give statements."

"That's fine, guv, but listen, these are my wife and kids. We, uh..." - my voice faltered. Don't cry you berk! – "I, uh, haven't seen them for about ten years. I, uh..."

"Rhona!" he called out to Wattsie. "Detective Sergeant Watts will make sure your family get in one of our cars. They can come to Tonbridge station too. But we'd better get you there straight away."

I told the kids to go with Wattsie and aimed a hopeful smile at Kara, who smiled back, without betraying the smallest indication of forgiveness. Well, it was a big ask, as people say these days, and there was a lot to forgive.

I got in the back of an unmarked car and drove past. Katie made a 'call me' gesture. I gave her a thumbs up and mouthed 'tomorrow...call you tomorrow.'

Not that I did.

There were a lot of civilians in the lanes around the farm, flocking like hungry carrion crows to the scene of the chaos. Among there were around thirty 'Broadies' chanting "Baker back inside!" repeatedly. They looked like a lynch mob. Uniform were trying to stop them from scrapping with a small, hostile group of heavy-looking South Londoners who were booing and threatening them. John was in the car behind mine and as he passed fights erupted, with the Broadies, who were in superior numbers, getting the upper hand.

I found out later that the Londoners were just an advance party. Minutes after we'd gone, Slobberin' Ron turned up with a coach-load, followed by a dozen cars. There were the Hogans, the O'Learys, the White brothers from Woolwich, Big Jim Cheetham, Mad Mickey Wharton, Martin Sporrell, an aggressive gooner. As they spilled from their vehicles the Broadies turned to flee – only to see another dozen or so geezers on blue and white customised scooters coming down the lane towards them from the opposite direction. These were the self-styled Millwall Mods – a gang of Scooter Boys from genteel Cobham in Surrey, Baker fans to a man. They caught the Broadies in a pincer movement and the cops, now outnumbered themselves, left them to it.

81

Tuesday's newspaper headlines were classics, my favourite being the *Star*'s BATMAN CAVES IN – one of the Tonbridge CID boys had told the hacks our nickname for Stevens. The *Mail* weighed in with FARMER FUHRER while the *Sun* had a great holiday shot of Charlotte in a bikini headlined BIRD OF PRAY, and promised 'Tomorrow – Inside The Bible Bunker'. Although by Wednesday, her secret sex-life had been exposed by a number of young men who called various news desks in pursuit of cash. Even the *Mirror* couldn't resist the obvious BIBLE BONKER headline, although the *Star* added 'And Batman's Bonkers' in smaller type, resulting in official complaints from Mental Health charities.

The Wednesday papers made horrible reading for William Broadwick, as the *Mail* published the first part of his wife's buy-up. It ran for five days, ending in the *Mail On Sunday*. No social embarrassment, no marital indiscretion was felt to be too small to leave out. The below the belt references to his manhood and stamina would not have made any man happy. "Broad wick?" tweeted TV comedian Jimmy Carr. "Never has a surname proved more ironic."

82

June 2013. Essex.

SO what can I tell you? Me and Kara have got back together. It was hard to get her to forgive me and trust me again, but it's all down to sincerity really, and as Bob Monkhouse used to say, once you can fake that you're laughing. Seriously, we've been together half a year. I don't know if we'll last but it feels right. I love being with the kids, learning about what makes them tick. Alfie's like me, he's going to be a proper charmer when he's a bit older. And Courtney Rose will break some hearts, you mark my words.

I never did call Katie. I didn't see the point. Besides, I don't think she's been that happy lately ever since some wicked bastard grassed up her Dad to Immigration and the Inland Revenue. I wonder what no-good, double-dealing crafty bastard could have done that....

The tax evasion stuff didn't do Ken McManus any harm, but his political mates weren't too chuffed to hear he'd been running his businesses on illegal immigrant labour. I don't suppose it sits that well with those 'Send 'em back' policies. I don't study politics, as you know, but I hear that the fledgling Hope & Progress alliance fell apart quicker than a clown's kitchen fitted by Frank Spencer.

Ken going down was the final straw, after the Broadwick fiasco. My own encounter with them confirmed my previous views on politicians. Most of them can neither be trusted nor believed...which is why I'm voting UKIP next time. Love England, hate bigots – that's me.

Broadwick himself experienced the most spectacular fall since Felix Baumgartner. It wasn't the Gulliver Stevens case that did for Our Willie, it was a nasty scandal of his own making. The way I hear it, he got fed up with the girlfriend, dumped her and tried to get back with his missus. It might have been love, but I can't help feeling that looming divorce settlements and his pension pot were bigger considerations.

Up until then he'd been doing pretty well for himself too. Broady's column had been snapped up by the *Telegraph* and he was lined up for a safe Tory seat in the Home Counties. But shortly after he went home to the wife, *Panorama* got hold of this tape of him coming out with a string of vile anti-Semitic garbage that only Hamas or Mel Gibson could have loved. Apparently one of his old schoolmates had secretly taped him. Got it all down on a microcassette. He was bang to rights. It damaged the movement badly but it crucified poor old Broadwick. Talk about fisted by fate. He lost his job, his column, his house, and the wife left him again so that divorce settlement is still looming after all. But hey, never say never, give him a couple of years and maybe he'll wobble back on *I'm A Celebrity...Get Me Out Of Here* or some such shit, sucking kangaroo balls for a second shot at national infamy.

Broadwick's bit on the side, Jackie Sutton, has done very well for herself though. A couple of well-judged appearances on *Question Time* and *Newsnight* in the wake of last year's antics saw her praised by the *Sunday Telegraph* for her skill in 'sugaring the pill of inequality and humanising the face of privilege.' The Prime Minister likened her to "Supermac in Olivier Strelli," although I reckon old Boris was more on the ball when he drooled that she was "the next Margaret Thatcher with the Iron Lady's brains and the looks and class of a young Grace Kelly." Either way, she's got herself that safe Conservative seat instead of Willie boy, and looks a shoe-in for the next election. People who know about these things reckon she'll get fast-tracked up to the Cabinet within eighteen months or so of getting in.

The Gulliver Stevens case is still going through the courts, but Gary Shaw tells me the old man will end up in Broadmoor and Charlotte will probably walk. She was smart enough to let her old man take all the blame – apparently she was one of his victims all along. He'd brainwashed her from an early age, and besides, according to all the available evidence, he was the one who committed all the murders. She may have aided and abetted under parental duress but nothing tied her to the actual killings – and only me, her, her father and the dead knew different.

What can I tell you about Johnny? Everything he said would happen in his life has happened or is happening. He's currently executive producing the movie of his own story, called *Johnny Too Bad*, and he's shacked up with this posh publishing totty with a double first from Cambridge and an old man who's a Labour peer. They're living over Shoreditch way. This year he's likely to gross more than Uzbekistan. John says he's gone legit. Only time and tax returns will tell if that's for real. An old rock writer called Garry Johnson has rushed out a cut and paste biography called *John Baker: Criminal Class*, sub-title: *The Rise, Fall & Rise Again of a London Legend*.

I got to know Mick Neale – our saviour! – really well over the past few months, so well in fact that I've asked him to work with me. He's still a bit reluctant – he keeps saying that he prefers good, honest manual labour because it gives the brain some peace. But I think he'll come round. Now him and Thelma are an item, he'll need more dough coming in, and the two of us just seem to click. There's an old Irish saying, 'a beetle knows another beetle', which just about sums it up. You always know when you've met a kindred spirit. I feel like I've known him all me life.

I've already set up the business – yeah, no corporations for the new wave sons. I've got my own office with a sign on the door and everything. I love it. It says: Harry Tyler, Private Investigator. And okay, it might have seemed a bit more glamorous and exotic if it was based in Brooklyn rather than Blackfen, but I've got a gut feeling about it. I reckon it's gonna work. The phone is ringing already. It's all good.

Glossary of Slang Terms

Apples - £20 notes (rhyming slang; apple cores = scores)
Ag – trouble, short for aggravation
Aris – arse (rhyming slang; Aristotle = bottle, bottle and glass = arse; see Queen Mum)
Banged up – imprisoned
Bang to rights – caught red-handed; guilty
Barry – a big woman (rhyming slang, Barry McGuigan = big'un)
Battle-cruiser – pub (rhyming slang, boozer)
Bent – Crooked or stolen goods
Bent – gay (see iron)
Beer tokens – pounds sterling
Billy – amphetamines (rhyming slang, Billy Whizz)
Bird – time in prison (bird lime = time)
Blade-runner – someone transporting stolen goods.
Blag – to rob, originally a pay-roll or money delivery in a public place.
Blagger – a robber
Boat – face (boat race = face)
Bob Hope – cannabis (rhyming slang, dope, see also puff)
The boob – prison.
To boost – to hot-wire a car.
Boracic – skint (rhyming slang, boracic lint).
Bottle out – to lose one's nerve (see brick it).
Brass – prostitute (see also Tom, dripper)
Brick it – to bottle out.
Britney Spears – ears
Brown bread – dead (rhyming slang)
A bullseye - £50
A bung – a bribe
Bushel – neck (rhyming slang, bushel and peck; see also Gregory)
Butchers – a look (Butcher's Hook, rhyming slang)
Canister – head (see Swede)
Carpet – three months imprisonment
Cash and Carry, commit – suicide (rhyming slang, hari-kari)
Charlie – cocaine, see also Chas, sherbet, marching powder, nose-bag, Gianluca, Ying, gear, King Lear).

Chavvy – a child (Romany)

China – mate (rhyming slang, china plate).

Chiv – a knife.

The Church – Customs & Excise (C of E)

Clean – innocent.

Clobber – clothes (see also schmutta)

Cobblers – rubbish (rhyming slang, cobblers' awls = balls)

A cockle – £10 (rhyming slang, cockle and hen).

Collar felt – to be arrested, as in "He had his collar felt")

The Currant – The *Sun* newspaper (rhyming slang, currant bun)

Dabs – finger prints.

Daisy – a safe-breaking tool

Darby – belly (rhyming slang, Darby Kelly)

Dave's mate – cocaine, from Chas and Dave, as used in the phrase "Is Dave's mate about tonight?"

Dipper – a pick pocket.

The dog – the telephone (rhyming slang, dog and bone).

Doris – a woman.

Dot – rotten (rhyming slang, Dot Cotton)

A drink – a bribe, ranging from a drink to a nice drink to a handsome drink.

Dripper – see brass.

Drumming – house-breaking.

An earner – easy money.

Elephants – drunk (rhyming slang, elephants trunk; see also Brahms & Liszt – pissed; all archaic)

Eyetie – Italian

Feds – the police

Fence – a receiver of stolen goods

The Filth – the police (see also Old Bill, cossers, rozzers, Plod, bogeys)

Firm – a gang

To fit-up – to give or plant false evidence.

Flowery – cell (rhyming slang, Flowery dell)

Four-be – a Jew (rhyming slang, 4 be 2)

In the frame – to be the prime suspect.

Frankie – cut-throat razor (rhyming slang, Frankie Fraser)

A friend of ours – one of us. A friend of mine, means he seems OK but hasn't been fully referenced.

Gaff – a house, see also drum and gaff of a gaff (a mansion)

The Game – prostitution, as in on the game

Gary – toilet or anus (rhyming slang, Gary Glitter = shitter)
George Young – tongue (rhyming slang)
Gianluca – cocaine (Gianluca Vialli = Charlie)
To give a pull – to impart words of advice.
Goldfish, to slip her the goldfish – sex (see poger)
Gold watch – Scotch (rhyming slang)
Graft – work, or piece of villainy
A grass – an informer.
Gregory – neck (rhyming slang, Gregory Peck)
Grumble – vagina (rhyming slang, grumble & grunt)
Gypsy's – a piss (rhyming slang, Gypsy's kiss; see also slash, lash and Jimmy, from Jimmy Riddle - piddle)
Half-chat – mixed race
Hampton – penis (rhyming slang, Hampton wick = prick)
Hand Grenades – AIDS (rhyming slang)
Hank Marvin – starving (rhyming slang).
Harry – semen (rhyming slang, Harry Monk = spunk)
A Henry – an eighth of an ounce of cannabis, from Henry VIII
An ice cream – a man/geezer (rhyming slang, ice cream freezer).
Iron – gay man (rhyming slang, iron hoof).
On your Jack – alone (rhyming slang, Jack Jones; also on your Tod, from Tod Sloan).
Jack and Danny – vagina (rhyming slang, fanny)
Jack The Ripper – stripper (rhyming slang)
Jacks - £5 (rhyming slang, Jack's Alive)
Jacksie – arse.
Jamjar – car (rhyming slang)
A Janet – a quarter of an ounce of cannabis (rhyming slang, Janet Street-Porter = quarter)
Jiggle – someone French (rhyming slang, jiggle and jog = frog)
Jivvle – a woman (dismissive term)
Joe – a Pakistani (rhyming slang, Joe Daki)
Johnny Vaughan – porn (rhyming slang)
K - £1,000.
K – Ketamine (also Special K)
Khazi – toilet (see Gary).
Khyber – arse (rhyming slang, Khyber Pass)
A Kim Jong-un – a wrong'un
Kosher – the real thing.

A long firm – a business set up and allowed to run over a fairly lengthy period with the sole intention of defrauding creditors.

On the Lash – a drinking session

Mangled – drunk

Manor – neighbourhood

To mark yer cards – to give advice.

Minces – eyes (rhyming slang, mince pies)

A monkey – £500.

Moody – fake.

A mug – a stupid person (also Muppet).

To mulla – to beat up.

Mutton – deaf (rhyming slang, Mutt and Jeff)

Ned – TV (rhyming slang, Ned Kelly = telly)

Nigerian Lager – Guinness.

A nonce – child sex offender.

North and south – (rhyming slang, mouth)

Nugget – a £1 coin

Oedipus – sex (rhyming slang, Oedipus Rex; archaic)

Oily – cigarette (rhyming slang, oily rag = fag)

OP – observation post

Orchestras – testicles (rhyming slang, orchestra stalls = balls)

A parcel – a consignment of stolen goods.

Patsies – piles (rhyming slang, Patsy Palmers = Farmers, Farmer Giles = piles)

Pet the poodle – female masturbation (also beat the beaver, hit the slit, juice the sluice, bash the gash, slam the clam)

A Peter – a safe.

Pete Tong – wrong (rhyming slang)

Pigs – beer (rhyming slang, pig's ear = beer, usually on George Raft – draft)

Plates – feet (rhyming slang, plates of meat)

Poger – to make love to, aggressively, as in 'I pogered the granny out of her'

A pony - £25 (also macaroni).

Pony – rubbish (rhyming slang, pony and trap = crap)

Pop – to pawn (rhyming slang, popcorn = porn)

Porkies – lies (rhyming slang, porky pie).

Puff – cannabis (also dope, Bob Hope, grass, blow, wacky baccy, ganja, weed, Beryl Reid, pot, the magic dragon).

Pukka – authentic (see Ream).

Queen Mum – the anus (rhyming slang, Queen Mum = bum; see Aris)

Rabbit – talk (rhyming slang, rabbit and pork)

Raspberry – disabled person (rhyming slang, raspberry ripple – cripple)

Ream – the real thing, or of good quality (see Pukka)

On the Rock 'n' Roll – unemployed (rhyming slang, dole)

Rosy – tea (rhyming slang, Rosy Lee)

Rubber – pub (rhyming slang, rub-a-dub)

Ruby – curry (rhyming slang, Ruby Murray).

Salmon – erection (rhyming slang, salmon and prawn - horn; also lob-on)

Saucepan – child (rhyming slang, saucepan lid = kid)

Schnide – fake (see also Sexton Blake)

Score - £20 (see apple).

See You Next Tuesday – a cunt

Septic – an American (rhyming slang, Septic Tank)

A sherbet – a cab (rhyming slang, sherbet dab)

Silvery – a black man (rhyming slang, silvery spoon; see also Feargal Sharkey)

Skin and blister – sister (rhyming slang)

Slag – a person with no principles.

Slaphead – a bald man, one who wears the pink crash helmet

A slaughter – a safe place to dispose of stolen goods, short for slaughter-house.

Smack – heroin (also horse, H, junk, skag, shit, brown, Harry, the white palace, the Chinaman's nightcap.)

A smudger – a photographer

Sniffer – a reporter (rhyming slang, sniffers and snorters = reporters)

A sov - £1, from sovereign.

SP – information, from starting prices.

Speed – amphetamines (see Billy)

Spiel – patter.

Squirt – ammonia in a bottle.

A stewards – an investigation, from steward's inquiry.

A stretch – one year in prison.

Strides – trousers

Stripe – to cut the face with a Frankie or a chiv

Surrey Docks – syphilis (rhyming slang, Surrey Docks = Pox)

Swagman – a dealer in cheap goods

Swede – head (see canister)

A syrup – wig (rhyming slang, syrup of figs)

Taters – cold (rhyming slang, taters in the mould; also brass monkeys from 'it's cold enough to freeze the balls off a brass monkey).

Tea-leaf – thief (rhyming slang)

Thrupennies – breasts (rhyming slang, thruppenny bits – tits; see also Earthasm Eartha Kitts, and Bristols, Bristol Cities – titties)

Tiddlies – Chinese people (rhyming slang, tiddly wink)

Tin-Tack – sack (rhyming slang; see also the Spanish Archer – El Bow).

Tits up – to go wrong or pear-shaped.

Tom – jewellery (rhyming slang, tomfoolery)

Tom – defecate (rhyming slang, Tom Tit = shit; see also a Forrest, Forrest Gump = dump)

Tool – a weapon

Vera – gin (rhyming slang, Vera Lynn)

Weasel – coat (rhyming slang, weasel and stoat)

A whistle – suit (rhyming slang, whistle and flute)

Wipe his mouth – to put up with the situation.

Wrong 'un – bad or untrustworthy person.

Wutherings – tights (rhyming slang, Wuthering Heights)

Appendix

When part one of this trilogy, *The Face*, was originally published in 2001 it had unexpected consequences. For starters the *Sun* sacked me. As I'd been with the paper off and on since 1985 and had been writing the *Bushell On The Box* TV column for them since 1987, this seemed like an extreme, not to mention unreasonable, over-reaction. So why did it happen? Chiefly because the *Daily Star* had serialised the novel. The serialisation had nothing to do with me whatsoever; my publisher John Blake did the deal with them while I was on holiday. He also wrote to the *Sun* taking full responsibility for what had happened. It didn't make a blind bit of difference. The paper's management said that I should have known in advance that when I sold the book to Blake he would give the serialisation rights to the *Star* who in turn would publish it alongside customary digs about the *Sun*...So basically I should have been Mystic Meg.

The *Sun*'s long-forgotten Editor at the time had actually promised to serialise the book himself, but then claimed he objected to a passage where my fictional gangsters have a pop at Lorraine Kelly on GMTV. They refer to her as "the Paisley pig." I have since apologised about this as I understand she comes from Arbroath.

It's hard to believe this is the truth however, as the Editor knew about that passage in the book at the launch, yet didn't change his mind about promoting it until ten days later. But if we do take him at his word, what does it say about him? That the editor of a national newspaper was so befuddled he actually believed that every line of dialogue in a work of fiction must reflect the opinion of the author. These were ruthless villains with unpleasant views; I no more share their thoughts than I spend my spare time pulling off bank jobs. Perhaps he also believed that Harry Potter really does magic. I'm fairly sure some pretty serious wand-polishing went on in his office.

The first I knew about the serialisation was when my friend Dale Winton called me at about 8.15am on the day it began. "Dear boy," he said. "Have you see the *Star*? You should!" I went and bought the paper from Woolworths, and was bemused. John Blake had just told me that he'd just asked them to review it!

I rang up two solicitors that morning (my old pal Henri Brandman and Gary Jacobs who I'd met on a few TV shows) to ask them what I could do to prevent serialisation. They said nothing, but at least I had a go which is more than the *Sun* ever did...

The resulting news story got more column inches than the book itself did. The *Star* was naturally delighted, pulling in quotes from celebrities and running a feature on an Essex pub full of *Sun* readers hoisting high the serialisation. Meanwhile, Matthew Norman in the *Guardian* (of all places) ran a doomed campaign to get me re-instated describing me poetically as the paper's exiled dauphin.

It was quite ludicrous and at the time baffling, but it all seems funny looking back at it now. For starters I work from home. On that first Monday I got a call from the Editor's PA asking me to come into the office, and when I got there he asked me to go home again. He called me in just to send me home! Other than that, he refused to speak to me. He never once asked me for my side of the story.

It was pretty hot that summer and I used to joke that to cool down I would pop down to Wapping just for the chilly reception.

I went through the internal appeals procedure believing the truth would out but it was farcical. Only Kafka would have been impressed. It seemed to me that they had made a decision and were just trying to retrospectively construct a case to justify it.

In the end most of the charges that were levelled against me were thrown out, so all they could sack me for was, as I said, for not knowing in advance that the book would be serialised elsewhere if they happened to change their mind about plugging it.

This they called "gross misconduct" which made it sound like I'd flashed the canteen staff, rather than simply signed a publishing contract eleven months before.

I should point out that a) throughout that entire period, the paper's top executives knew I was writing the book for Blake and indeed had actively encouraged me to do so; b) the deputy editor's soap star boyfriend put himself forward to play Harry in a TV adaptation should one ever happen; c) I had signed literally scores of similar contracts with TV companies and book publishers before and d) there was a list of News International employees as long as a spaniel's ears who had done similar deals with John Blake without getting sacked for it...

It was blatantly unfair and the only surprise was at the time this surprised me. Looking back though, I don't regret any of it. Parting company, however rudely, turned out to be liberating.

Not everyone took such an active dislike to *The Face*. Bob Monkhouse and Billy Murray loved it. In fact, Bob was so outraged on my behalf that he rang up the *Sun* newsdesk several times using a Scottish accent to ask them where my column was. "I'll not be buying this rag again," MacBob informed them, and I don't believe he ever did.

Elsewhere Roy 'Pretty Boy' Shaw called *The Face* "completely bloody brilliant." Barbara Windsor dubbed it "raw, funny and authentic" and added "I can't wait to see the movie." The *Spectator* quoted Johnny Baker's political views with approval. Caroline Aherne reviewed it semi-warmly, with a stiletto edge of facetiousness. More positively, Jonathan Ross called it "excellent pulp fiction." His better-looking brother Paul raved about the novel too. Billy Murray, Dave Legeno, Ross Kemp and Craig Fairbrass all separately expressed strong interest in appearing in a big screen version, which as yet has not happened although it has been much discussed.

One enthusiastic Scottish producer I met up with in 2003 was well up for making it but ended up doing time for fraud, so I'm glad I let him buy the drinks. Six years later I was contacted by a company in Los Angeles who specialise in selling the film rights to books to Hollywood. Nothing came of that either, which is probably just as well – I'm not sure how the slang would have gone down in California. As least with a British production I might have half a chance of keeping the local colour in, and the story on the rails.

Harry Tyler's saga continued in *Two Faced* (published 2004), which was both a prequel and a sequel, and has come to a halt here. Thank you to all the readers who bothered to contact me and tell me what they thought of Harry's adventures, and especially to those who badgered me to complete the trilogy. This book is down to you. I enjoyed getting re-acquainted with the characters; and who knows if enough of you buy it, the halt might just be a temporary one.

Garry Bushell, August 3rd 2013

Also by Garry Bushell

GARRY BUSHELL'S ESSAYS ON THE MOD REVIVAL
FROM THE 1979 FRONTLINE.

The Mod Revival of 1979-80 put life and laughs into an increasingly grim post-punk UK scene. Snobby music press hacks tried to write it off as a hype manufactured by the film industry to plug Quadrophenia. Not true. The roots of 'New Mod' were actually in The Jam and their All Mod Cons album which inspired a generation of teenagers to embrace the joys of Fred Perry's, Harrington jackets, Vespa's - and powerful songs with great tunes.

Garry Bushell was the first rock writer to cover the scene, reviewing the Purple Hearts, the Jolt, the Chords and Secret Affair in rapid succession between 1978 and 1980. He was also the only one who gave the young backstreet bands a fair hearing.

This is his funny, informative and affectionate history of the rise and fall, rebirth and lasting influence of the Mod Revival as it happened. Including all the major bands and most of the minor ones. Available for the first time ever in book form, includes never before seen photographs of The Chords, The Jam, The Purple Hearts and Secret Affair.

Also by Garry Bushell

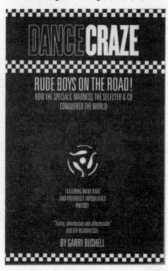

"Your last chance to dance before World War Three" *Specials* singer, Terry Hall called it. An exaggeration of course, but 2-Tone did serve up the most perfect pop music since Trojan reggae had dominated the UK Top Ten a decade before. And the bands kept coming - *Bad Manners*, *The Beat*, *The Bodysnatchers*. Even *Judge Dread* made a comeback.

Garry Bushell, who wrote the original Dance Craze magazine, was the first rock writer to see the *Specials* live, the first to interview *Madness* and the first to watch the bands attempt to export their magic to the USA. This is his funny, informative and affectionate history of the rise and fall and rise again of the Rude Boys.

This is the heavy, heavy monster book, the nuttiest read around! It's also the only introduction you'll ever need to the boss sound of the 1980s! Available for the first time ever in book form, includes many unseen photographs.

Time for Action and Dance Craze are published by

Countdown Books

Coming soon from Caffeine Nights

The UK's most downloaded sports title of 2012!

APPEARANCES CAN BE DECEPTIVE - as Paul Jarvis of the National Soccer Intelligence Unit is only too well aware. He knows that Billy Evans is no ordinary Cockney lad made good. He's also a thug, a villain and a cop killer. Jarvis just hasn't been able to prove it...

Yet.

So when Jarvis discovers that Evans is putting together a hooligan 'Super Crew' to follow the England national soccer team to Italy, he feels sure he can finally put Evans behind bars - if only someone can infiltrate the group and get him the proof he needs.

But nothing is ever that simple. The Crew believe Evans is just out for a full-on riot. Jarvis thinks he's trafficking drugs. But Billy Evans is always one step ahead. He has another plan. And it will be catastrophic for everyone concerned.

EXCEPT HIM

The Official Novelisation from the Movie

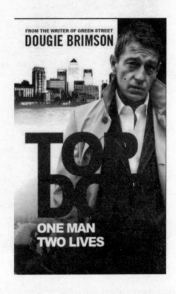

Sequel to the best-selling thriller, The Crew. Soon to be a

major motion picture starring Leo Gregory

GANG LEADER Billy Evans has ruled his turf in London for more years than he can care to remember. So long in fact, that even he realizes that things have become a little too easy.

So when an old adversary reappears on the scene, Bill sees a golden opportunity to not only reassert his authority, but to have some much needed fun.

Yet all is not as it appears. For this new enemy is far more powerful than any Billy has ever had to deal with before and he's about to discover that he's finally pushed his luck too far.

But this time it isn't the law that he has to worry about, it's something far more dangerous.

Published by Caffeine Nights Publishing Spring 2014

The Official Novelisation from the Movie

Now a major motion picture starring Danny Dyer

George never meant to kill the thief – he was just defending
his shop from the jacked up kids trying to rob him. Break the
kid's jaw maybe, but not kill him. Later the doorbell rings and
in revenge the gang swarm into George's house, beat him
senseless, rape his wife, tie them up and set fire to them.

It isn't long before Jimmy Vickers, George's son, is on the trail
of the gang who murdered his parents, exacting his own kind
of chillingly brutal justice. Jimmy is an interrogation specialist
for the military in Afghanistan who knows more than he
should. With the police closing in and his own regiment also
determined to stop him, the body count mounts up. Jimmy
creates a media frenzy - London's first vigilante of the 21st
Century - but will his devastating course of action spell the end
for the woman he loves?

Published by Caffeine Nights Publishing October 28th 2013

More Great Titles from Caffeine Nights

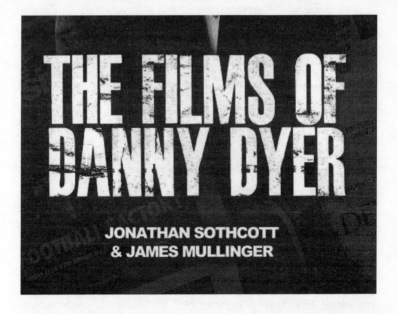

Danny Dyer is Britain's most popular young film star. Idolised by Harold Pinter and with his films having taken nearly $50 million at the UK box office, Dyer is the most bankable star in British independent films with one in ten of the country's population owning one of his films on DVD. With iconic performances in such cult classics as The Business, The Football Factory, Dead Man Running, Outlaw and now Vendetta, Dyer is one of the most recognisable Englishmen in the world. For the first time, and with its' subject's full co-operation, this book chronicles his film career in depth, combining production background with critical analysis to paint a fascinating picture of the contemporary British film industry and its brightest star. Packed with anecdotes from co-stars and colleagues, as well as contributions from the man himself, The Films of Danny Dyer is the ultimate companion to the work of Britain's grittiest star.

Published by Caffeine Nights Publishing 18th Nov 2013

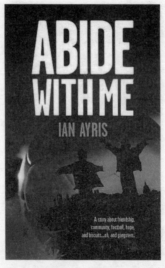

Two boys. John and Kenny. One streetwise and football mad, the other cold and unfathomable. It's nineteen-seventy-five. The heart of London's East End. As John celebrates the Hammers beating Fulham in the Cup Final, Kenny tumbles out the door of the new people's house across the street having taken a beating of a different kind. When the new school year begins, John befriends Kenny, defending him from the ridicule of his classmates. But when you become mates with someone as odd, as downright terrifying as Kenny, nothing is ever straightforward. Amidst the turbulent years of late seventies London, the lives of John and Kenny spiral out of control. They meet again, years later, and local villain, Ronnie Swordfish, is after Kenny's head. All John can do is watch. Kenny, he ain't saying a word. He never does. So when Ronnie gives the order to fetch his three foot Samurai sword, John thinks the game's all but up. Thing is, he don't know the half of it...

Abide With Me is a story of football, friendship, and hope.

And gangsters. A story of how two boys walked blind into the darkness...and emerged as men..

More Great Titles from Caffeine Nights

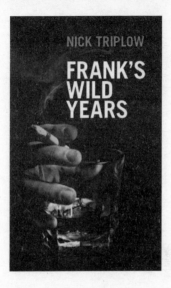

Frank's Wild Years is a story of betrayal and last chances at the frayed and fading edges of the south London underworld.

IN THE TWILIGHT days between Christmas and New Year, ageing Frank Neaves is about to drink away his last tenner in a Deptford boozer. A former friend and associate of long-dead local villain Dave Price, Frank's scotch-soaked meditation is interrupted when it's discovered that Carl, Price's son and the pub's landlord, has disappeared leaving an oblique one line note for barmaid, Adeline.

After a visit to Carl's mother, Rose, they discover he has gone to Hull to bring his young daughter, Grace, back to south London to celebrate New Year's Eve. Adeline knows this means coming up against the malevolent James O'Keefe, Carl's ex-wife's new bloke and small time crook. Certain of a violent confrontation that the Carl can't win, Adeline persuades Frank to join her and together they take a slow train for Humberside.

Over the course of the next few days, Frank, Carl and Adeline each have a chance to redeem past mistakes, none more so than Frank, whose past comes back to haunt him in ways he could never have imagined.

More Great Titles from Caffeine Nights

Released from prison, and hacked off with a life of petty crime, Jim takes a new job: contract killing. But, what happens when your first hit fails? When the target has a heart attack before you can pull the trigger?

Charlotte, a keen city worker, jumps to the victim's aid in the busy streets of South London. Should Jim carry out the contract and also kill Charlotte? What he shouldn't do is help her to save his life; that really won't impress the new boss.

The man saved, Jim has a massive problem; he has to repay his advance, and also his boss expects compensation. Immediately.

With seven days to make ten grand, Jim starts a one-man crime spree in the heart of the financial district. But will his budding relationship with Charlotte prove to be a help or a hindrance as he struggles to stay alive?

More Great Titles from Caffeine Nights

Introducing Joe Geraghty

Described by the Hull Daily Mail as Hull's answer to Ian Rankin, Nick Quantrill has crafted one of the grittiest British detectives in the UK today in the shape of Joe Geraghty.

The Crooked Beat

When Joe Geraghty's brother finds himself in money trouble, it's only natural that he turns to the Private Investigator for help. But when it relates to a missing consignment of smuggled cigarettes, it's not so easily sorted. Drawn into the murky world of local and international criminals around the port of Hull, Joe Geraghty knows the only way to save his brother is to take on the debt himself. But as he attempts to find a way out of the situation, the secrets and conspiracies he uncovers are so deeply buried in the past, he knows he's facing people willing to do whatever it takes to keep them that way...

More Great Titles from Caffeine Nights

The Fourth D.I.Dylan novel from writers RC Bridgestock.

RC Bridgestock are script consultants on ITV's award winning drama, 'Scott & Bailey' and BBC's new crime drama 'Happy Valley'.

PEOPLE GO MISSING EVERY DAY BUT IN SEVERE WEATHER THE NUMBERS INCREASE.

When Kayleigh Harwood, a young hairdresser, is reported missing by her mother in the worst blizzards Harrowfield has experienced in years, D.I. Jack Dylan and his team are called in to assist. Kayleigh's car is found abandoned with her mobile phone inside but there is no sign of her. Clothing is found on nearby moorland and a search of the local quarry begins.

The investigation turns to a loner living in a dwelling close to where Kayleigh's car was found.

As the snow thaws human remains are found and Dylan's boss Chief Superintendent Hugo-Watkins thinking the two incidents are linked calls out the entire Major Incident Team, much to Dylan's disbelief.

Meanwhile Dylan's wife, Jen, becomes distracted and distant as unbeknown to Dylan her ex fiancé is in their midst and stalking her.